D0350569

LOVE
BOMB

JENNY McLACHLAN

FEIWEL AND FRIENDS
NEW YORK

A FEIWEL AND FRIENDS BOOK
An Imprint of Macmillan

Printed in the United States of America by R. R. Donnelley & Sons Company, Harrisonburg, Virginia. For information, address Feiwel and Friends, 175 Fifth Avenue, New York, N.Y. 10010.

Library of Congress Cataloging-in-Publication Data is available.

ISBN 978-1-250-06149-2 (hardcover) / ISBN 978-1-250-08031-8 (ebook)

Our books may be purchased in bulk for promotional, educational, or business use. Please contact your local bookseller or the Macmillan Corporate and Premium Sales Department at (800) 221-7945 ext. 5442 or by e-mail at MacmillanSpecialMarkets@macmillan.com.

First published by Bloomsbury Publishing Plc

Book design by April Ward

Feiwel and Friends logo designed by Filomena Tuosto

First U.S. Edition—2016

1 3 5 7 9 10 8 6 4 2

fiercereads.com

FOR MY MIGHTY
AND AMAZING GIRLS,
NELL AND FLORA

1.

I sing Betty to sleep.

Lined up on her changing table is a box containing eighty-seven "true lilac" envelopes, a fountain pen, and a pad of Vergé de France ivory paper. I pull off a sheet and run my hands over the cool, blank surface. My skin is as pale as the paper. I take out a new envelope and look at Betty lying in her crib.

She's started blowing dream bubbles, her lips opening and shutting, and her cheeks are a rosy pink. The thin curtain lifts on a breeze and her whisper-fine hair trembles.

I haven't got much time.

Plumface is 15!, *I write on the envelope. Then I pause. I feel so tired. Through the open window, I hear the neighbors' boys scream as they jump in their kiddie pool. Then I enclose my words with a big cartoon heart, smooth out the sheet of paper, and start to write . . .*

LATER . . .

Holy smoke . . . school actually *started* seven minutes ago, and here I am, playing with Legos. I shake Frosted Flakes into my mouth, glug down some warm milk, and abandon my last birthday presents. I'm actually going to have to *run* to school. At least I get to try out my brand-new Puma sneakers . . . gold stripe!

I fly down the road and cut through Sunrise Senior Living, glancing down every now and then to admire my retro feet.

"Get off the grass!" yells an old lady from her kitchen window. I smile and wave, then run across the parking lot, sending a flock of baby seagulls squawking into the sky.

Clambering up the wall by the art block, I manage to hover on the top for a second before losing my balance and crashing down on the other side. A last-minute roll saves me from injury, and I lie on the ground, catching my breath, kind of regretting the warm milk.

"Explain yourself, Betty Plum!"

Oh, bum. I know that voice.

"Hello, Mrs. Pollard," I say sweetly, scrambling to my feet. My head teacher sucks in her breath and grips her clipboard with white fingers. As usual, I have filled her with rage, but for some reason she's suppressing it. And that's when I realize she's not alone. Standing behind her, leaning against the fence, and staring up at the sky is a boy.

At least, I think he's a boy. He's almost too gorgeous to be real. It's like a movie star has dropped onto our playground. My heart goes crazy and I blush. I *never* blush, and the only other time my heart's felt like this was when I was shocked by a toaster. I look at the new boy again and see pale skin, a mesmerizing mouth, and wild dark hair. Vampire, I think. No, Betty, stupid, vampires don't exist. He's just supernaturally hot. My heart pounds as if it's trying to escape from my body. What's happening to me?

The new boy yawns, and I gaze at his long, curling lashes. Wow. They are *Beautimus Maximus*. They make me feel faint! And then I realize what this means. Something momentous has just occurred: I like the new boy! This is literally the first time in my life I have fancied someone *real*. Unlike my friend Kat, I don't wander through school, tongue hanging out, drooling over "the talent" and giving boys scores out of ten . . . until now, that is.

Because New Boy is definitely a ten out of ten.

"I'm still waiting," says Mrs. P., tapping her clipboard with her pen.

I can't speak. I've just FALLEN IN LOVE, and now my mouth won't work. How can Mrs. P. fail to register the epic sexual tension in the air? Doesn't she feel awkward?

"Sorry, ma'am," I finally manage. "As I was running to school, I found an old man out walking in his pajamas, so I took him back to his old folks' home." She doesn't look very impressed, so I add, "He had *bare* feet."

"Hmmm," says Mrs. P., eyes narrowed.

"It's true!" I'm indignant because this did actually happen . . . several weeks ago. "He gave me this to say thank you." I pull off the newsie cap I'm wearing and shove it under her nose.

"Hmmm," she says again, making a few notes on her clipboard. "You may have noticed we have a visitor, Betty." Slowly, oh so slowly, the new boy lowers his eyes from the sky. "This is Tobias Gray, and he will be joining your class."

"Toby," he says, his deep voice tickling my stomach.

"What's that?" Mrs. P. says.

"I'm Toby."

"Right. Make Tobias feel welcome, and join me at lunchtime to discuss"—she wiggles her finger in little circles, indicating my purple nails, bracelets, sneakers, and newsie cap—"*everything.*"

"But, Mrs. Pollard, it's my birthday!" She is unmoved and turns and walks away.

Toby straightens and looks in my direction. I freeze. His eyes are a startling pale blue and more catlike than Mr. Smokey's (who is actually a cat). A smile plays on his lips, and the hairs on my arms stand on end. Then, as quick as a flash, he winks at me before following Mrs. P.

I've never been winked at before. Not a boy-girl wink. I watch him go. His pants are nonregulation and too skinny, and he's rolled up his blazer sleeves. Mrs. P. hates us doing that. He's so tall that as he passes the trash cans he has to duck to avoid being hit by a low-hanging branch that reaches into the playground.

He looks back at me.

My mouth is hanging open, and my hands are pressed into what I believe is my heart area.

He smiles and turns away.

Not cool, Betty. Not cool at all.

Somehow I manage to return to planet Earth and stagger to art. After giving Miss Summons a lame "late bus" excuse, I go and find Kat doing something disgusting with human hair. Bea is nowhere to be seen. "Miss Summons's son works at a hairdresser's," explains Kat, her face wrinkled with disgust as she sprinkles blond fluff onto a pile of white glue. Her perfect shell-pink nails push stray hairs back into the heart she's making. "Apparently I'm experimenting with the fragility of the human body."

I drop into the seat opposite her. "It looks like you're experimenting with being a serial killer," I say. "But forget about hair, Kat—look at me." I point at my face with both fingers so she can't miss it. "Do I look different?"

She studies me, wrinkling up her nose. "Do you look fifteen and not fourteen?"

"No, but thanks for remembering."

"Are you a little red because Mrs. P. told you off in front of that *lush* new boy? I saw through the window."

"No, Kat, I am a little red because someone has just made my heart explode, and I believe I have *fallen in love.*"

"I knew you and Mrs. P. had a special thing going on, always hanging out together at lunchtime and after school—"

"Those are called *detentions.*"

"Joke, Betty," says Kat, grinning. "You like the new boy. Of course you do. He's eight and a half out of ten, totally gorgeous"—Kat disappears under the desk—"and so is this!" She pulls out a huge helium balloon. "Happy birthday, Betty! Look, Eeyore and Pooh are hugging Tigger. You're Tigger, I'm Eeyore, and Bea is Pooh."

I tie the balloon to the end of my hair, and we watch as it starts to drift toward the ceiling.

"Hey," she says, "it makes your hair float."

"Thanks, Kat," I say, and we smile shyly at each other. We are kind of newish friends, so this balloon is special. In our first art lesson, I volunteered to pose for figure sketching and did a series of demented poses. Only Bea and Kat laughed, even though they were *very* funny. I got sent out, but it was worth it because the three of us have been hanging out together ever since.

The timing couldn't have been better. My two so-called *best friends*, Charlie and Amber, had just abandoned me. At the start of term, Charlie went to live with her dad in Manchester, and Amber's parents sent her to a private school for a "fresh start," or possibly just to get her away from me.

"Kat," I say, pulling the balloon down, "I need your help."

She pushes her hairy art aside and makes her face look serious. "Go on," she says.

"So there's this new boy, Toby, and he looks *just* like a hot vampire." She nods. She understands—she's seen him. "He stared at me like he wanted to *devour* me." Kat raises her eyebrows in alarm. "Let me make this clear: I *want* him to devour me."

"But, Betty, you've never even kissed anyone . . . or had a boyfriend. I'm not sure you're ready to be devoured."

"I've never *wanted* to kiss anyone, but I think I do now."

Kat claps her hands with excitement. Finally, she can talk boys with me . . . her best skill. "Hey, Bea must be showing him around," she says. "She got told to go to reception."

"Good. He's safe for at least one hour," I say. Unlike me, as Kat so loudly pointed out, Bea has a boyfriend. But I'm still worried. "Soon Pearl Harris and Jess Cobb will sniff him out and pounce on him. He's the only boy I have ever liked in my entire life, so I can't let Pearl steal him from me. Plus, I saw him first."

"I'm not sure you can bag boys," says Kat. Then she starts rummaging through the hair on the desk in front of her. "Okay, so who am I?" She holds all the hair on her chin and says, "Ohhhh, I wuv you, Toby!"

"Are you me with a beard?"

"Yes!"

Then we have a hilarious art lesson making hairy things.

Bea joins us as we're leaving. "That new boy is so *rude*," she says, all shocked and pink and Bea-like. "He followed me around the school, always walking three steps behind, and he kept *sighing*." She does a pretty good impression of Toby staring up at the sky, rolling his eyes, and doing a bored groan. "So I took him to see the school piglets, but he wasn't even interested in them."

"Weird," says Kat. "They are cute piglets."

The three of us link arms and head toward math, the

balloon bobbing between us. Even though we're new friends, we're old friends, too. When we were in nursery school, we were in a gang called the Ladybirds, along with Pearl Harris, who has since become a man-eating bully. The Ladybirds drifted apart, but now we're almost back together.

"Bettyass is in lovass with that rudass boyass," Kat tells Bea.

"I can understand what you're saying, Kat," I say. "Your secret ass-language is rubbishass."

"It's coolass," says Kat.

"No, it's notass," I say. "Anyway, he was probably sighing because he was thinking about me." Kat and Bea laugh. I laugh, too, so they know I'm joking.

I'm not joking.

Please, please, god of love . . . Eros? Venus? Whatever, *please* make Toby Gray speak to Betty Plum *today*. It would be the most awesome birthday present ever.

Thanks for nothing, Erosnus.

Despite stalking Toby all of lunchtime, I leave school without exchanging a single word with him. I start to walk home, reminiscing about the way his powerful fingers tore off a Twix wrapper, and just as I'm thinking about the lazy way he played soccer with the juniors, I spot Bill waiting for me outside the grocery store.

"Bill, you freak!" I yell across the road. He looks up and smiles. Bill's my best friend, even though, as his name suggests, he is *un hombre*. He goes to the Catholic boys' school, Cardinal Heanan, which is why right now he's wearing a hideous maroon blazer and a stripy tie. His uniform clashes very amusingly with his wild blond hair and deep tan. Bill's a surfer, a *wind*surfer, to be precise—apparently there's a difference—and he spends every available moment on the sea.

I cross the road. Despite his alarming appearance, I'm still willing to be seen in public with him.

"Hey," Bill says, throwing a Tesco bag in my direction. "Got you a present."

As we walk toward my house, I look inside the bag. "Yuck! What is that?" I pull out a tiny but very realistic horse mask. "Is it for a baby?"

"It's a cat mask for Mr. Smokey," he says. "Now you can have a tiny horse running around your house." I stroke the mane. "Don't you like it?" he asks, frowning.

"Are you joking?" I say. "I *totally* love it." I start to tell Bill about my other birthday presents. "Dad got me a Lego set, as usual, the *Millennium Falcon*, although it clearly says for ages nine to *fourteen* on the box. I need you to help me make it."

Bill and I turn the corner, and I gasp. Toby is slouched at the bus stop, still hanging out with his new soccer friends. Instantly my heart speeds up, and I feel my cheeks burn.

"Bill," I say, stuffing the mask back in the bag, "when we go past those boys, promise not to let me look weird."

"Honestly, Betty, I can't promise that. Why?"

"Because you see that tall boy with the floppy dark hair?"

Bill scans the group of boys. "The one doing rapper hands?"

"That's him," I say. "I want to impress him."

"Why?"

"Errch, don't make me spell it out."

"What are you talking about, Betty?" he asks. We are getting really close to the bus stop.

"Because I *like* him," I hiss.

"Oh," says Bill, and he goes quiet. This is a strange moment for us. It's the first time I've ever mentioned liking someone who is real and not a singer or an actor or Flynn Rider from the Disney film *Tangled*. We watch as Toby shows a boy something on his phone.

"You mean you *like* him?" Bill asks.

"Yes."

"Him?"

"Yes!"

"I suppose he does look a little like Flynn," he says.

"Exactly. Now shut up." We are walking past the bus stop. "Hey, Toby!" I say. My words come out loud and hysterical. Startled, he looks up from his phone and stares at me. His eyebrows raise and then he smiles. His smile makes me dizzy with happiness, and I have to say something to him, something that will make him fall in love with me. "Getting the bus?" I ask.

"Er, yeah," he says, turning back to his friends.

"Getting the bus?" says Bill loudly. "Brilliant!"

I try to smack him with my bag, but he just catches it and pulls me around. Unfortunately, what with all his windsurfing, Bill has powerful upper-body strength, and he swings me deep into a bush.

"I think I look weird," I say.

"Just a bit," he says, pulling me out. "Sorry about that."

Bill is so at home at my place that he's making toast before the kettle's even boiled. I go to get some jam and see that Dad's left a birthday message on the kitchen table—*Hippo Birdday, Betty!*—and I mean he's *literally* written it on the table. I started this when I was six when I wrote *Daddy smells ugly* with a permanent marker. There's not much room left now.

"What do you want on your toast?" asks Bill.

I throw him the jar, and he catches it with one hand. Our mums met in the maternity unit at the hospital and instantly became BFFs. They made sure Bill and I did everything together: breast-feeding, naps, potty training, oh, and baths, of course, loads and loads of naked baths.

Obviously, they took hundreds of photos to record the humiliating early days of our friendship.

Then, just before I was two, my mum checked out on the world. It wasn't her fault. She had cancer.

I drop tea bags into mugs and pour in the boiling water. Now Bill and I are the BFFs. "What's this?" I say, picking up my favorite mug, the one with GROOVY GRANDDADS written on it.

"It's definitely a mug."

"No, *this*." I point at a pale pink smudge on the rim. "Is that *lipstick*? I know Dad's been home because he's written on the table." I sniff the smudge. "It smells like lipstick. Bill, do you think Dad dresses up as a woman while I'm at school?"

"Or, maybe," says Bill, licking the jammy knife, "he made a woman a cup of tea?"

"What?"

"Maybe your dad's got a girlfriend."

"No way," I say, and then I start sniffing. "Does the house *smell* different?" I sniff my way into the hallway, then back to the kitchen. "I think it smells like a shop in Brighton. The kind of place that sells crystals or beads." The smell is making me feel funny, like someone's broken in. Our house should smell of curry and paint, not flowery incense.

"Your dad's got a hippie girlfriend, Betty. It was going to happen one day."

I shake my head. "Bill, the idea of Dad sneaking a

pink-lipstick-wearing hippie girlfriend in here and making her a cup of tea in *my* mug on *my* birthday is just"—I try to think of the right word—"wrong. Honestly, we tell each other everything. I'd know if he had a girlfriend. Anyway, we're happy on our own."

"Is that why I'm not invited to your birthday tea tonight?"

"Yes! You'd ruin it. It's perfect with just me and Dad . . . no offense."

"You've got a card you haven't opened here." He taps a purple envelope with his knife.

"Oh, that's Mum's birthday letter."

"Sorry," he says. "I've got butter on it." He tries to rub it off with his sleeve. "Aren't you going to read it?"

"Not this year."

"Why? You used to love them."

"Not really. She wrote them for a baby. They're all, 'You can say *bird*, you hate bananas, you did a massive poo.' . . . They've got boring."

Bill passes me my toast and looks at me with his serious gray eyes. He's waiting for me to explain. But I don't want to talk about Dead Mum's letters, not today. I hardly ever think about the fact that I don't have a mum, and it's only on my birthday, when I get one of her letters, that I realize I'm missing something.

"Come on," I say, picking up my tea. "If we're building a naked Lego man, we need to get a move on."

"You said we were making the *Millennium Falcon*."

"I lied," I say, leading him into the front room.

After Bill's gone, I keep working on the naked man's tiny toes. Suddenly I hear Stevie Wonder's "Happy Birthday" come on in the kitchen, and then Dad bursts into the room singing along and doing a truly shocking dance routine.

He does a couple of circuits of the room, then puts his hands out to me and says, "Dance with me, birthday girl!"

"No way," I say, but eventually I let him pull me up, and then I dance with him just like I did when I was little, standing on his toes and going round and round in a circle.

For dinner, Dad makes my special feast of macaroni and cheese and baked beans (the baked beans are combined in the cheesy sauce), and then we eat my M&M's-decorated cake and watch *Jailhouse Rock*. Watching an Elvis film is a birthday tradition, and, as usual, Dad sings along to all the songs while I groan and roll my eyes. I love it really.

Finally, I gather up my presents. I'm ready for bed.

"Good birthday, Plumface?" asks Dad. He's sprawled on the sofa, still wearing his work jeans.

"The best," I say, from the corner of the stairs. "I love the Legos."

"You're never too old for Legos, right?"

"Right, Dad."

"I see you got started on it. It's looking good."

So funny. If Dad looked closely, he'd notice the *Millennium Falcon* has a lovely pair of brick buttocks.

"Night, Bumface," I say as a special treat. He loves it when I call him this. Me, Mum, and Dad: Plumface, Mumface, and Bumface. These names take Dad back to such a happy place.

At the last minute, he says, "You saw your letter from Mum?"

"I don't want it." My presents wobble in my arms.

"Betty." He comes to the bottom of the stairs. "It's the *last* one."

"What do you mean?"

"You haven't got any more birthday letters. That's the last one she wrote. She only managed to write them up to your fifteenth birthday."

"Oh," I say.

"Are you okay?" he asks.

"I'm fine, Dad," I say. Then I struggle my way up the stairs into my bedroom and drop the presents on my bed. I flop down after them.

The last one.

I wasn't expecting that.

When I was little, I got Dad to read my mum's first letter to me so many times that now I know it by heart.

Dear Plumface,

Whoop, whoop . . . you are two! I wonder what you will see today. Daddy, obviously, but maybe you'll get a surprise and see a big ginger cat or the moon or Auntie Kate. At the moment these are your favorite things, and you can say all of them. This is what they sound like: ginge, moo, and ka ka. This last one is funny because it's German for poo! I hope it's sunny and Daddy puts lots of M&Ms on your cake. Don't put them up your nose like last year. . . . If you do, Daddy will have to suck them out again.

Love you always,
Mumface xx

But *the last one*.

I suppose I thought Dad had loads of them stacked away in his wardrobe and that I'd go on getting them forever. I pick up one of my presents from Dad, a bottle of Wild Bluebell cologne, and I spray some on my wrist. It smells yummy, of flowers and woods, but I feel a bit sick. Perhaps hot chocolate *and* chocolate cake wasn't the greatest idea.

I lie back and turn the glass bottle around in my hands. This isn't a usual Dad present . . . could it be one of Dead Mum's suggestions? She has done it before. Along with the letters, she gave Dad a list of present ideas. With perfect timing, Mr. Smokey (*twelfth birthday: gray kitten*) slips into my room, trots to the bed, and leaps effortlessly onto my stomach.

He pushes his head against my hands until I rub his nubbly velvet chin. I stare at the glow-in-the-dark stars on the ceiling while he kneads his nails into my top. Dad makes the best birthday cakes, my friends make my hair fly *and* throw me in bushes, and just the thought of Toby Gray's smile makes me tingle. I should be purring like Mr. Smokey right now.

But something feels wrong.

A knot of worry is hidden deep inside me.

I shut my eyes and try to discover what it is, but everything gets confused . . . Toby's blue eyes falling on me, tracing a curve of pink lipstick on a white mug, and, resting against the bread bin in the kitchen, the purple envelope with a heart drawn round the words *Plumface is 15!*

"Hey, Mr. Smokey," I say, picking up his paws to get his attention. "Ever fancied being a horse?"

"Meow," he says, which obviously means, *Yes, Mistress, it's my life's ambition!*

2.

The next morning, all my worries disappear when Mr. Simms makes an exciting announcement in study hall.

"Listen up, guys!" He's perched on the edge of his desk, tie loose, sleeves rolled up, doing his cool-teacher thang. "It's time for our tenth- and eleventh-grade Autumn Celebration." A ripple of interest runs round the room. The Autumn Celebration is legendary. Not because of the quality of the performances, but because of the imaginative ways students get inappropriate material into it. Last year, Bea's boyfriend, Ollie, sang "Da Ya Think I'm Sexy?" with his band and gyrated in Mrs. P.'s face for the entire track. When they signed up, they said they were going to do a folk song about a lonely fisherman.

"This year," says Mr. Simms, "Mrs. Pollard has

specifically said: *no rude songs*. It's happened too often, and we are onto you." I might be imagining it, but I'm sure he pauses here to stare at me. "If you want to take part, put your name on the music notice board. No auditions. We're all about equality here . . . but definitely *no* rudeness."

I turn to Kat and Bea. "We are going to do *total* rudeness, agreed?"

"Do you remember two years ago," says Bea, "when Beth Fisher sang 'Peacock' and Mrs. P. let it through because she thought it was about wildlife?"

We smile at the memory. "And finally," says Kat, "we can take part because we're sophomores!"

"Let's do some blue-sky thinking, girls," I say, rummaging in Bea's bag for her felt-tips. I write *Rude Ideas* in huge bubble letters across a page in my Dennis the Menace sketchbook.

"Don't be mad," says Bea, "but I can't do anything. I'm going to be jiving with Ollie, and we're only allowed to perform once."

Bea jives, like old-style rock-and-roll dancing, and she's amazing at it. With Ollie, she entered a TV talent show, and since then they jive at every possible opportunity, and sometimes when they really shouldn't be doing it at all. I should have known "Bollie" would be jiving at the Autumn Celebration.

"I do have a *very* rude idea, though," she says gleefully.

I look up from the cartoon rabbit I'm drawing. "My dad's band, the Weirdie Beardies, play hokum, which is old blues music where the lyrics sound all innocent but actually, they're *really* dirty."

"I'm liking it already," I say, abandoning my bunny. "Go on."

"So these songs are all on my dad's last, ahem, 'album.'" She tucks a stray curl behind her ear. "'Let Me Play With Your Yo-Yo,' 'My Pencil Won't Write No More,' and, my personal favorite, 'Hot Nuts, Get 'Em from the Peanut Man.'"

"Yes, I vote 'Hot Nuts'!" screams Kat. Mr. Simms tries to stay cool, but his anxious gulp and glance at the door says a lot.

Suddenly, there's a shriek from the corner of the room. We look over to see Pearl Harris, clapping her hands and screaming in a totally girlie way . . . okay, in a totally *Kat*-like way. Her friends collapse in laughter, then she stares, stone-faced, straight at Kat. A Pearl Harris stare is quite something. She's clearly got it in for Kat at the moment and still hasn't forgiven her for sticking up for Bea last year.

Quickly, I suck in my cheeks and throw her snooty, cold face right back at her, nose stuck up in the air, eyes wide and glaring. She's not quite sure what to do next; after all, I'm imitating her for imitating Kat. . . . Where will this end? She decides to go with mouthing "Skank" at me.

"Now, that, girls," I say, "is an example of hypocrisy."

Pink cheeked, Kat carries on, but this time, she speaks quietly. "Betty, I *have* to do a performance as part of my music final. 'Hot Nuts' could be it. I'll play the guitar, which, as you all know, is an awesome skill of mine, and you'll sing." She pauses here and looks at me. "You really can sing, Betty."

"I can, but I don't. I'm going to play the keyboard, which is a weak skill of mine, and you are going to sing."

"But I can't sing and you can." Kat's perfectly shaped eyebrows are raised in expectation, and her wide blue eyes are gazing at me. "C'mon, Betty," she pleads. "It will make up for Jesus."

Will she ever forgive me for Jesus?

When we were eight, I had a tantrum just before our school nativity and screamed until Miss Hooker gave me the role of Mary and the Jesus doll. Unfortunately, Kat was supposed to be Mary and I was a crappy old star. To be honest, it kind of destroyed our friendship for the next seven years and kick-started the breakup of the Ladybirds.

"You know I don't like singing, Kat," I say, making her roll her eyes. My mum was a singer with a band called the Swanettes. She adored the blues singer Bettye Swann and all things sixties, hence my rather *special* name. It's generally agreed that I've inherited her *lovely, beautiful, magical* voice that has the power to reduce my relatives to tears. It's kind of spooky. "I do like the idea of 'Hot

Nuts,' " I say cautiously, "but can't I just play the tambourine or something?"

" 'Hot Nuts'?" says Bea. " 'Hot Nuts'?! No way will Mrs. P. agree to that one."

"Okay. We do the pencil song," I say to Kat. " 'My Pencil Won't Write No More.' Mrs. P. will think it's something to do with English."

"But you *have* to sing so I can play the guitar," says Kat, looking desperate. "If I don't do a guitar performance before the end of the year, I have to perform on my own in a sophomore assembly. I'd rather jive than do that . . . no offense, Bea."

Bea just smiles dreamily and starts to entwine flowers around the large *HOT NUTS* I've written across the middle of the page. Kat's made her think of jive and her *boyfriend*, and it all makes her amazingly happy. I have a little wiggle of my own happiness as I roll the words *boyfriend* and *Toby* around in my head, enjoying how good they sound together. Maybe it's worth breaking my no-singing rule if it means I get to bewitch Toby with my magical voice.

I make a bold decision. "I will sing hokum at the Autumn Celebration," I announce. "Sign us up, Kat. We're a band!"

Kat and I agree to rehearse at her place on Sunday. Then, with the help of Kat and Bea, I spend the rest of the day stalking Toby. To improve the quality of our surveillance, we go to the sophomore office and tell the secretary that Mr. Simms needs a copy of Toby's schedule. Two minutes later, we know where he is every minute of the day.

I spend the next few days trailing him. Soon I find out his favorite drink is grape soda and that he always gets to PE on time and to English late. On Tuesday I discover he likes playing Fruit Ninja on his phone. To find this out, I have to stand very close behind him in the lunch line. My nose actually *touches* his blazer. I could have licked him. All right, I did lick him, but only a tiny bit and just to make Bea laugh.

I'm so busy loitering outside the boys' locker room on Wednesday that I lose track of time, and Toby, and get to science late. I burst into the room to find the class already paired up and dissecting dead fish. In the corner, I see Kat trying to stick scales in Bea's hair.

"Sit with the new boy," instructs Mr. Brooks, barely glancing up from his computer. Mr. Brooks's words have a powerful effect on me. Heart hammering and body tingling, I make my way to the back of the room. Finally, I'm going to get to speak to Toby again.

He is rocking back on his stool, his arm stretched across the lab table, watching me as I walk toward him. His eyebrows are raised as if he's amused by some secret thing.

"Hi," I manage to say as I sit next to him.

"All right?" he says, tilting his head to one side.

Say something, Betty, say something! "It looks like we're a couple," I finally manage. Wrong thing! Abort, abort. "I mean, a pair, partners . . ."

"Life partners?"

"Science-experiment partners," I say desperately.

"Got it," he says, smiling. Then he pushes a petri dish toward me. It contains a small green fish that's speckled with yellow spots. "We need to find a worm in its gills," he says. I take in his dark lashes and high cheekbones, and I notice a small hole in his top lip where he must have taken out a piercing. Suddenly, I realize I've been staring at him for far too long.

He catches my eye and his smile grows.

I blush and look away only to spot Bea and Kat watching us gleefully. Kat mouths something, which might be "Oh my God," then they both shut their eyes and start French-kissing the air. Bea gets really into it, running her hands up and down her body and sticking her tongue out. It's quite a sight.

Toby catches the end of their performance. He looks at me and frowns.

"My friends," I say, quickly picking up a pair of tweezers and poking around in the spongy gray flesh, desperately trying to hide the blush that's spreading powerfully across my face and down my neck. Suddenly, and inexplicably, I say, "I'm coming to get ya, worms!" in a southern accent. Like a cowboy. This is terrible. I. Must. Stop.

Talking. "Where are those critters?" I mutter, still with the accent. Yikes! I glance over at Toby. He's started texting under the table, possibly ignoring me.

He puts his phone away, and I show him the little worm I've found.

"Nice work, Betty," he says. The sound of my name on his lips makes me melt. "We've got to fill this in," he adds, reaching across the table, his arm brushing against mine.

"Right," I say, forcing myself to look at the work sheet he's holding. It looks like Mr. Brooks has asked one of his children to draw a picture of a fish. All around the blobby image are boxes and arrows.

"I think he wants us to write the names of Muppets in the boxes," I say.

"Definitely," says Toby, and he starts writing. I glance over his shoulder and help him out when he runs out of names. In box eight he writes *Vanilla Chinchilla*.

"That's not a Muppet," I say.

"Vanilla Chinchilla is the name of a legendary band," he says, his face lighting up. "*My* band!" On the back of the work sheet, he draws his band's logo for me and explains the Vanilla Chinchilla "sound." I watch as his beautiful hands move across the paper.

"Who's in the band?"

"Well, like, no one except me," he admits. "But I'm auditioning for a drummer and bassist this afternoon. And I'm looking for a singer."

"I can sing," I say. The words just fly out of my mouth.

"Yeah?" He looks at me and nods his head. "You should totally audition, B-Cakes. Vanilla Chinchilla is gonna be sick." Okay, so *sick* is a funny word to use, but *B-Cakes* . . . I have a nickname. Toby has given me my very own nickname! He rummages about in his bag. "Here." He passes me a rubbery key ring. "Have a bit of Vanilla Chinchilla merchandise. That's going to be worth something one day." He nods seriously.

"Cute," I say. "It's a mouse."

"No. A chinchilla."

"Eating an ice cream."

"A *vanilla* ice cream."

"Got it," I say. I clip the key ring to my bag. "So how come you moved schools?" I think I'm getting the hang of this talking-to-a-gorgeous-boy thing.

"Because," he says, resting his face on his hand and gazing at me, "I did some *bad* stuff."

"Like putting a piglet in your teacher's car?" I ask, deciding to run some of my own "bad stuff" past him. "Or taking your PE class back to your house for snacks during cross-country? Or henna tattooing the new seventh graders?"

"Just stuff," he says, smiling. "Would you like to see an example?"

I shrug. "Sure."

"Look around you, B-Cakes," he says, indicating all the students sitting in the classroom. "Who do you hate?"

I study the backs of heads spread before me. I don't *hate* anyone. Toward the front are Kat and Bea, their faces turned away from me. Suddenly, Kat dissolves in laughter, and I wonder what Bea said. Then my eyes fall on Sam Oakley, who is sitting near them. I don't really like Sam. "That boy with the black hair," I say, pointing. "He says 'Rah!' in little kids' faces and laughs at my duck backpack . . . it's got a big beak."

"I'm gonna destroy him," says Toby, picking up the scalpel. I'm quite relieved when he bends over the fish and gently presses the fish's white eye out of its socket. What he's doing is pretty gross, but such is the power of his handsomeness that all I really notice is how great his forearms look with his sleeves rolled up.

Next, he walks to the front of the room, scanning the tables as he goes. After picking up a textbook from Mr. Brooks's desk, he returns to his seat, pausing for a fraction of a second in front of Sam. No one sees what he does next except me. In one swift movement, he drops the eye into Sam's open water bottle. I don't know what to think. It's such a revolting thing to do, but he did it for me. Toby walks back to his seat, smiling a bad smile. When he sees the shocked look on my face, he laughs.

"Put down your pens," calls Mr. Brooks. "Betty, can you give me your answer to question one?"

I look down at our work sheet. "Fozzie Bear," I say. Mr. Brooks is not amused and reaches for a "Bad News" sticker to put in my planner. Amazingly, I'm saved by Sam Oakley, who suddenly leaps to his feet and sprays a fountain of water over Mr. Brooks and his stickers. The lab erupts into laughter, and I think of all the times Sam Oakley has laughed at other people, just to make them feel small.

"Nice bad stuff," I whisper to Toby.

I catch up with the girls at the end of the lesson, and we walk out of school together.

"Like, *wow*, Betty," says Kat. "He is *into* you!"

"You think so?"

"He really laughed when you said Fozzie Bear," says Bea.

We stand outside the gates, waiting to go our separate ways. I want to keep talking about Toby, but more than anything I want to be alone so I can run over everything he said to me. "I'll see you two tomorrow," I say. "I'm going to go home and lie on my bed and think about Toby . . . and his blue eyes . . . and his muscular chest."

"*You've* got a muscular chest," says Kat.

I start to walk away. "You've got a muscular *face*!" I yell over my shoulder, and then I grin. I grin all the way home as I wonder how I might have got myself into two bands when I never even wanted to be in one, and I grin as I walk down my road, remembering the way Toby called me B-Cakes.

The sight of my house in the middle of our cul-de-sac, with its purple front door and overgrown yard, makes me even happier. The kids from number seven are climbing on the tree on the shared grass, and they call out to me. I can see their dad playing with his model train set in his garage. Best of all, Dad's yellow bike is resting against the side of our house. Dad's got his own decorating company called Man with a Van . . . but get this, he hasn't got a van. Instead, he's got a bike and a trailer he hitches to it. He says that if he was called Man with a Bike and Trailer, he wouldn't get any business.

I let myself in, find him in the kitchen, and give him a massive hug. I smell coffee and paint thinner, the nicest Dad smell in the world.

"I've got a bit of news," says Dad when I step back. I can tell by the way he says this that he's practiced how it will sound. He's aiming for casual, but he misses, big-time.

"What?" I start to rummage about in the fridge. I think I know what's coming, and I don't want to hear it.

"Just that I'm going out on Saturday night, if that's okay, with a friend." A friend. A friend? Why doesn't he just say it? He means *girl*friend. I hear the dishes rattle in the sink. "She's someone I met through work," he says. "I painted her yoga studio."

Bill was right, a *hippie* girlfriend. I keep quiet.

"Her name's Rue."

Rue? Rue! That is so *not* a name. I know I'm supposed to say something now, something like, "That is *so* great, Dad!" but I can't. Instead, I go with staring at a blueberry yogurt in the fridge. I wonder if he was thinking about her when we were eating my birthday cake. . . . Maybe she chose my perfume. I'm throwing it out.

"Look, Betty," Dad says. I slam the fridge shut and turn to face him. "I knew you'd find this hard. It's been just the two of us for so long."

His words make my heart feel like a small, hard stone. I can't stop the horrible thoughts that pour through me like a film on fast-forward: I see *Rue* curled up on the sofa in my spot, Dad taking *Rue* camping with us, *Rue* making herself breakfast in our kitchen . . . wearing Dad's painty shirt . . . and *nothing* else.

"It must have been *terrible* for you," I blurt out. "I didn't realize you *hated* being with me so much, just the two of us for *so* long!" Tears appear from nowhere.

"Betty," says Dad, putting out his arms. Normally I love hugging Dad. He stands there in his faded band T-shirt waiting for me to come to him. Around his wrist he's wearing two friendship bracelets I made for him when I was seven. He's never taken them off. Not once.

"I *hate* this, Dad," I say, turning away and walking out of the room. "I wish you'd never told me!" I run up to my room, banging the door shut. Then I lie on my bed, hugging Mr. Smokey and making his fur all tufty with my tears. Eventually, he wriggles out of my grasp and sits by the door until I let him out.

I curl up on my bed and stare at the shut door. Now I'm all alone. My eyes fall on a purple envelope sitting on my bedside table. Mum's birthday letter. The last one. I don't know when Dad put it there. I pick it up and feel its weight in my hands. I find a gap in the envelope flap and push my finger into it. Downstairs, I hear Dad's voice talking on the phone. He could be chatting to anyone—Gramps, a customer, one of his mates—but I can't stop myself from thinking *he's talking to her.*

I throw the letter across the room, and it lands in a pile of junk by my wardrobe.

Next, I put on my big green headphones and listen to the Clash. Dad hates this album. I turn the volume up loud until the music makes my insides shake. After a few seconds, I reach over to my ancient hi-fi and pull the earphone cable out.

Now the whole house shakes.

3.

On Saturday morning, Dad goes Poo crazy. That's right, *Poo*. She is totally asking to be called Poo by having a name that rhymes with it. Usually Saturday breakfast is my favorite time in the week: Dad makes pancakes, I choose some groovy music, Mr. Smokey watches us suspiciously, and Dad comes up with a plan for the weekend. Previous Pancake Plans include:

1. Getting the ferry to France because we realized we were out of Nutella and it's cheaper over there.
2. Taking Mr. Smokey to the seaside so we could see if he liked paddling (negative).
3. Seeing how far we could cycle before it got dark (53.5 miles—Croydon).
4. Visiting six historical properties in one day in an

attempt to take a photo of a ghost (no ghosts, but we ate a lot of cakes).

5. Visiting six historical properties in one day dressed as ghosts (with Nanna and Gramps).

The Poo assault starts the moment the pancakes hit the pan.

"You remember I'm going out tonight?" says Dad.

"Flip it, Dad."

"So Rue's going to pop in at six, just to say hello and show her face—"

"Seriously, Dad, they're burning."

"—and then we're going to that veggie Indian place I took you to in Brighton. I think she'll love it."

"Have you seen the maple syrup?" I ask, banging the cupboard door shut.

"She's a pescatarian."

"I put maple syrup on the shopping list," I say. "No way am I having honey."

"*Pescatarian* means she eats fish," says Dad, putting a new bottle of syrup on the table. "Then we might go to a comedy club, but I'll be back late. Is that okay?"

"Dad, you've got to see this." I thrust my phone in his face. "It's a baby sneezing into his birthday cake!"

He takes my phone out of my hands and drops it on the table. "She's coming over, Betty. I want you to say *hello* and *smile* and be *nice*."

"Fine," I say in a normal voice, but I have absolutely no intention of saying hello, smiling, or being at all nice. To punish Dad, I text my friends all through breakfast. He hates this but lets me do it because he's trying to keep me sweet for this evening.

This is what I send:

Just found out dads got a heinous hippie girlfriend am supposed to meet her tonight YUCK!!!!!!!!!!!!!!!!

Here's what I get back:

Kat: **Babe you wanna come here and go in the sauna? Luv Kitkat**

Bea: **Poor Betty ☹ Jiving tonight can you come? Xxxxxb PS Just made a yum lemon drizzle cake!**

Bill: **Big news . . . you ok? Come over to mine after windsurfing?**

None of these suggestions are satisfactory. If I leave the house, Dad might sneak Poo in. Instead, I decide to do something which is definitely very sane and normal. I barricade myself in my bedroom by pushing a chest of drawers in front of the door. I make sure I've got supplies—juice, crackers, and a banana—and I also take in a jug in case I need to pee. Then I sit on my bed and wait.

My bedroom matches my mood. Being a decorator's daughter, I was allowed to paint my room any color I wanted, and I went for blue. My ceiling is Inky Pool 3, my walls are

Skylight, and my door is Blue Lagoon. And it's messy. Mugs, abandoned cereal bowls, magazines, and clothes are scattered across the floor. I'm sitting in a big blue mess.

Just as the sky becomes a fraction darker than Inky Pool 3, a car sweeps to a stop in front of our house. I duck away from the window, turn my music up loud, and bury myself in my bed. As the doorbell rings, I pull a pillow tight round my head so I don't even know if Dad calls me.

After I've checked they've gone, I creep downstairs and make some cheese on toast. Then I sit among the junk in my bedroom and eat my crappy dinner. All I can think about is Dad and Poo nibbling on crispy pakoras, trying each other's sweet stuffed naan, and laughing about what a "terrible teen" I am.

Even thinking about Toby doesn't cheer me up. I've gazed at him a lot this week and even managed to speak to him a couple of times, but nothing has satisfied my monstrous Toby cravings. In fact, the more I have to do with him, the worse they get.

Among the tangle of clothes pouring out of my wardrobe is the newsie cap the old man gave me. I'm sure that wearing it will cheer me up. I tug at it and a landslide of sweaters, scarves, jeans, and bras spill onto the floor. Then I discover I'm holding a sock, not the newsie cap. I rummage through the clothes, and before I know it I'm organizing things into piles. I even have a trash pile and a charity-shop pile. One pile is particularly rectangular and purple, my Dead Mum letter pile. The deeper I get into my wardrobe, the more letters I find.

It's only when I've put everything back in the wardrobe, hung my three dresses on hangers, and thrown out the trash that I realize I still haven't found the newsie cap. Never mind. I haven't thought about Dad and Poo for at least an hour.

The only things left on the carpet are the letters.

I decide to arrange them in date order. I have fourteen. The first one I ever got has been read so many times, it's falling apart. The letter on the top of the pile is *the last one* and the only one I haven't opened. I turn it over and over. It seems heavier than the others, and the edges are crisp and sharp. Why did she draw a heart on this one?

I put the rest of the letters in the Puma shoe box that's been lying on my floor since my birthday, and then I climb into bed with the unopened letter.

Taking a deep breath, I run my finger under the seal and peel open the envelope. I pull out three sheets of paper.

Dear Plumface,

Today you are 15, but as I write these words, you're one and a half and a lunatic. Seriously, you eat flowers but only yellow ones. The only time you aren't being crazy is when you are asleep, like right now.

I've just done some math in my head—which is impressive as I only scraped a C in my math final—and

I've discovered something frightening. Something as frightening as finding a drooling orc under my bed who is panting and wants to eat me. If, by some miracle, you are unfamiliar with Dad's favorite book, The Lord of the Rings, *orcs are sentient beings bred for evil. So I've discovered something terrifying, and if you bear in mind I have terminal cancer, you'll realize I have a good grasp of frightening situations.*

A year ago, Dr. Harper told me that in a "best-case scenario" I might *have "twelve months to live." Then he did a wincey face that seemed to say, "Don't go booking any vacations for next summer!" Today, my twelve months are up, so it looks like my plan to write you a letter for every birthday of your life was unrealistic. I was going to do 120, in case you eat loads of raw veg and live to be ancient. So far, I've written fourteen.*

In the words of Dad when I told him I was pregnant: crapola.

Admittedly, when I decided to write 120 letters, I was taking a lot of drugs (prescribed), and I also decided to release an album and run the New York City Marathon.

I haven't sung with the Swanettes for months, and the last time I ran—from the kitchen to the living room when you bit Dingo's tail—I ended up on a drip. Every day I sleep for a few more hours, and this morning I couldn't eat my toast.

Betty, I love toast.

I am just so tired. I don't know how long I can keep going, even for you, my beautiful, wild baby.

So I have a plan. I'm going to hide some letters up in the attic in my Remington Super Smooth Ladies' Razor box. If you want to read them, you know where to look. If you don't want to read them, that's okay. I wasn't interested in anything my mum had to say when I was 15 (or 18, or 23, or 26). Either way, there's a good razor up there.

These letters are going to be different from the birthday ones. To be honest, I was running out of things to write, and sometimes it was difficult thinking of jolly things to say when my mood was really rather somber. Imagine it: Hey, Plumface, You are three! Just had chemo, and I've got rampant diarrhea, and my mouth is stuffed full of painful ulcers!

The letters in the attic are between you and me. I'm not even going to tell Dad they're up there, but I've made him promise to leave some boxes of stuff up there for you. They will be stories. Stories about me when I was your age. Stories about me doing all the things you are probably going to do. Stories even Dad hasn't heard . . . including the one about my first-ever kiss, history boy, and my scalp spot. There. That's called "a teaser." You see, even though your dad is quite simply the best, *he doesn't know what it's like to be 15 and a girl.*

For me, the most frightening thing in the world isn't a drooling orc under the bed, or even dying. It's knowing that I am leaving you, my baby, which is really the worst thing any mum can do.

If you would like to read my stories, Betty, they are my 15th birthday present to you.

Love you always,
Mumface xxx

Everything is silent in the room. I sit and stare at the letter. I know what Mum looked like; I've seen loads of photos—huge smile, swinging blond hair (dyed), freckles like mine—but, just now, I almost *heard* her. Usually when I read my birthday letters, they come from the past, but these words were whispered in my ear. Hairs prickle on my arms, and my throat feels sore.

I look up at the ceiling. Are Mum's letters in the attic waiting for me? Part of me wants to rush up there and find out, like I'm doing a treasure hunt, but something holds me back. What if she never managed to write them? What if Dad threw them out by mistake? Instead, I bury myself further into the bed and read the letter one more time.

I want to have a mum again, just for a few minutes.

I get to Kat's house early and discover her family doing squats in the garden. Seriously. Her mum, dad, and big sister are all exercising in skintight running spandex first thing on Sunday morning.

"Betty!" yells her dad, jogging over to high-five me. His slap is so enthusiastic, I fall off my bike. He helps me up. "We're competing in a Tough Mudder today!"

"Tough *what*?" I say.

"Mudder," says Kat's mum, panting. "It's the hardest endurance test *on the planet*."

Kat snorts. She's appeared at the front door. "It's jogging in *mud*, Betty." She's wearing shorts and a bra and holding a can of Coke. Kat may not share her family's love of exercise, but she certainly shares their love of hanging out naked. She claims they are "physically at ease" because her mum's Swedish, but her dad also seems to be a fan of nudity, and he's from Portsmouth. Last time I was round, he was doing tai chi in *very* loose yoga pants.

"Any chance I can persuade you and Kat to join us?" he asks. He straightens up and then starts touching his toes. "There were still a few places yesterday. . . ."

"As if, Dad," says Kat, rolling her eyes. "I told you. We're rehearsing."

"Don't whine, Kat," he says. His head appears between his legs. "Kids whine."

"Whatever," she says, turning round. "Come on, Betty. Let's leave these losers to it."

Her mum laughs as if Kat's just said the cutest thing, and then they all pile into a Range Rover the size of my bedroom.

"Help yourself to cinnamon buns, Betty," calls her sister as they pull out of the driveway. "I baked them this morning."

Kat's family is awesome. I leave my bike by the front door and follow Kat inside. I crept out early this morning, making sure I didn't wake Dad, then cycled along twisty lanes into the countryside. The crisp air and perfect blue sky made me forget all about Dad and Poo.

Kat's house is made entirely of pale wood and decorated in shades of white. I feel as if I make the place messy just by being in it, like an inky smudge on a sheet of paper. I run my finger along the edge of a smooth vase shaped like a drop of water and stare at a beautiful picture of the sea. Kat's mum painted it.

Kat settles in the den, slumped in a huge beanbag with her guitar across her knees. She's pulled on a sweatshirt. "Ready to do this, Betty?" she asks, strumming a few chords. "Let's nail this pencil song!"

And we do. Kat starts playing—she's obviously been rehearsing—and I pull out my lyrics. Right from the start, we sound good together. We practice for ages, having a few cinnamon bun/Toby analysis/jukebox breaks. That's right, Kat has a *jukebox* in her den, along with a pool table, a dance pole (her mum's), and, tucked away behind some sort of indoor tree, a sauna. This is the only den I have ever been in, but I think *den* must mean tons of cool stuff in one room.

The two of us make a good band, and by lunchtime we've come up with an arrangement we like.

"Let's run through it one more time," says Kat. "Then we can go into town and get KFC."

By now we're both standing, and I belt it out. Kat's plugged her guitar into an amp and starts improvising. To be honest, we forget all about the weenie jokes and get into the song. It's full of soulful chords, and the pitch suits my voice. Kat ends the song with a mad crescendo of strumming, and we do lots of whooping and *yeahs*!

After grabbing a couple of juices from the mini fridge, we crash on the beanbags.

"We weren't bad, were we?" she asks.

"Possibly, just possibly," I say, grinning at her, "we were *good*."

I roll off the beanbag and wander over to the baby grand. Did I mention the piano? Music is scattered across it. Kat's sister is an advanced piano player, which kind of puts Kat's intermediate guitar playing to shame. Suddenly, I spot a faded yellow music score. "No way!" I say, picking it up. " 'Then You Can Tell Me Goodbye' by Bettye Swann. My mum and dad named me after this singer."

"I can play that," says Kat, coming over.

"My mum was singing this song when Dad first saw her."

"Tell me," says Kat, sitting on the piano stool. "I love getting-together stories."

"Well, my mum was doing a mini tour with her band, the Swanettes, during her college vacation." Kat is watching me, wide-eyed. "So it's this warm summer's evening, and the Swanettes are singing at this pub, deep in the countryside and—get this—the pub is called the Falling Star." Kat sighs deeply. "My dad is sitting in the garden when he suddenly hears this beautiful voice drifting out on the rose-scented air. He follows the voice inside and discovers it belongs to an angel, otherwise known as Lorna. Their eyes meet, and she sings the song to him, as though no one else is in the room. Afterward, he buys her a pint of Harveys and some pork rinds, and they talk for hours as the sun sets over the fields . . . and the rest is history."

"That is soooo romantic," says Kat. "Except for the bit about the pork rinds. C'mon, let's recreate it." Kat sits down on the piano stool and opens out the music on the stand. She picks at the strings on her guitar, then starts to play the song that is so familiar to me I can't remember a time when I haven't known the words. It seems only natural to join in.

"Wow," says Kat, after the final note has faded out. "Are you sure you don't want to sing that at the concert? That was good, Betty. "

"No way," I say. "My dad would have a cow. It would be like the ghost of Mum had just been zapped onto our school stage."

"We'd better stick with the willy song, then."

We grin at each other, and I think how great it is to be here, with Kat, talking about willies. I gaze around the room. The walls are covered with photos of her mum from her modeling days in the eighties. You can see where Kat gets her cheekbones and lanky legs from.

"Have you ever seen such ugly clothes?" asks Kat.

"Is that a *plastic* dress?" I ask.

"Yep," says Kat. "And look at this. It's a *gold* shell suit."

"What's a shell suit?"

"Like a tracksuit made of silky underwear material. Mum got loads of freebies from designers. There's a room upstairs full of them: lace gloves, rah-rah skirts, Keds, boleros, shortalls, leg warmers. . . ."

"I don't know what all those things are."

"She's even got *ladybird* stilettos. C'mon. I'll show you."

Two hours later, we're heading toward Bea's house, eating fries and dressed as eighties supermodels.

"Fashion!" I yell, and Kat spins round and strikes a pose. Each time she does this, her poses get weirder. This time she's crouched down on the ground, pointing her milk shake up at the sky.

Somehow, Kat's managing to carry off the eighties look better than me. She's wearing a neon-pink jumpsuit, leg warmers, and the übergorgeous stilettos. Essentially, she looks like an eighties supermodel. I'm wearing gold rapper pants, a sweater covered with colorful licorice, and red pixie boots. Essentially, I look like a loser. Kat took some persuading—unlike me, she isn't familiar with the joys of parading around town in fancy costumes—but she knew she looked good and couldn't resist showing off her new look.

"Do you think Bea will want to hear our song?" she asks.

"Definitely," I say. I should add that Kat also has her guitar strapped to her back, and I'm riding my bike, very slowly. "It was her idea in the first place."

"We could go and sing to Bill," says Kat. I look sideways at her. She grins, then takes a long suck of her milk shake.

"Why do you want to show Bill?"

"C'mon, Betty. Bill's cutesome. He's a nine out of ten . . . maybe more." She gives me a shove, making me wobble on my bike.

"*Nine* out of ten? No way. Seven would be generous . . . and what's *cutesome*?"

"*Cute* plus *handsome* equals *cutesome* . . . equals Bill."

"Nope. . . ." I picture Bill's serious face, his messy sun-bleached hair. "I don't see it, Kat."

"Then you're blind."

"Fashion!" I yell, and Kat spins round, then peers at me over her shoulder, three french fries sticking out of her pouting lips.

We ring Bea's doorbell and smile in anticipation. Although her house is in darkness, we can hear jivey music playing somewhere. Suddenly, there's a patter of footsteps, and a small pink shape appears behind the glass. The mail slot is poked open by Bea's little sister.

"Who that?"

"Hi, Emma," says Kat, crouching down. "It's us. Can you open the door?"

"Okay," she says, then disappears. Several minutes

later, she returns with a collection of books. She starts to build them into a tower.

I shove Kat out of the way. Three-year-olds have no sense of urgency. "Hurry up, Emma," I say through the mail slot. "We look really stupid and it's cold."

"I'm too small," she says. I watch her add a few more books to her teetering pile, and then she climbs up. "That's better. I can do it now!" Her hand reaches toward the door handle, but then she stops. "Uh-oh."

"What?"

"I need to pee!"

And she's gone again. When she finally reappears, she's dressed as Iron Man.

"You look tough," I say when she finally lets us in.

"You look stinky," she replies. Ouch. "Bea and Ollie are in the kitchen," she says as she scampers back upstairs, karate chopping the banister and yelling, "Die! Die!"

Kat and I head toward the thudding of "Bim Bam Baby." As we get closer, we can hear panting and gasping. Now, if it were any other teenage couple behind that door, we might have knocked, but it's just Bollie—so we walk straight in.

Ollie is holding Bea up in the air in a position I can only describe as a double-hand butt grab. Next—I can't really tell how it happens—Bea is sliding between Ollie's legs and popping out the other side. The music stops and we clap. Bea looks so happy, her rosy cheeks could burst. Even though she's been applauded loads of times for jiving, she still loves it.

"What do you think?" asks Kat, spinning round.

"You look so cool," says Bea, examining the stilettos.

"Oh no, you don't," says Ollie, laughing.

Soon Bea and Ollie are sitting on the sofa with Emma wedged between them. Kat and I are ready to perform.

"Okay, Emma," I say, "this is a song about a pencil that doesn't want to do any more writing." I glance over at Kat and she nods. I take a deep breath, swallowing the last of my singing-aloud fears. Kat hits the first chord and we're off.

It doesn't sound quite as amazing as it did in Kat's den with her amp and the big acoustics, but our audience seems to enjoy it, and when we finish, Emma yells, "Again, again!"

We play it one more time, then Bollie show us a few new moves, and Emma sings a song about a "naughty gruff" which may or may not be about the Gruffalo. We all agree it should definitely be in the Autumn Celebration.

It's starting to get dark when Kat and I head home. We stand at the edge of the park, ready to go our separate ways.

"Thanks for singing with me, Betty."

"It was loads of fun," I say. We look at each other. It's so good to be back where we were before I stole Jesus. "Hey, I've got a question for you, Kat. It's a bit surprising."

"Go on."

"How do you kiss?"

Kat laughs. "You're right. I wasn't expecting that."

"It's just I think there's a chance that I might kiss Toby one day," I say, "and I don't want to look stupid."

"My sister told me that you just shut your eyes and let it happen. But you could practice on an apple with a wedge cut out of it."

"Really? That doesn't sound right. Isn't that just eating an apple?"

"You don't eat it—you *kiss* it. Mum recommended it. She's kissed loads of people, so she should know."

"It sounds a bit crunchy," I say, pushing off from the curb. "Laters, Kat!" She does a final "Fashion!" pose, and I cycle down the road. I can smell wood smoke, and my breath puffs out in front of me. "I'm going home to snog an apple!" I yell over my shoulder. Then the road dips, and I zoom down with a massive "Wahoooo!"

5.

The next morning, I "accidentally" run into Toby outside his homeroom.

"Oh, hi," I say, all surprised.

"Well, hello, Betty." He leans against the wall and fixes his eyes on me. We are standing close enough for me to notice that he has a darker circle of blue around the edge of his pale iris. I try hard not to stare. "You need to come to the hall after school to audition for Vanilla Chinchilla," he says.

"Really?"

"You'll be perfect. I've asked a few other girls to come along." *Other girls*? What does a few mean? Two other girls? Seven? Thirty-four? "Don't worry," he says, resting his hand on my arm, "I know you'll rock, B-Cakes. The moment you said you could sing, I wanted you in my band." He smiles and everything inside me trembles; then he lets go of me and strolls into his classroom, leaving me with a deliciously tingly arm.

I want to follow him, grab his hand, and put it right back on my arm, but even I have some dignity. I drift toward my homeroom, and slowly my arm returns to normal. My body has had a life of its own recently. Just this morning, when I walked past the attic hatch, the hairs on my arms prickled as I thought of Mum's letters hidden up there, and then, at breakfast, a hole appeared in my stomach when Dad made me promise to go to Pizza Express with him and Poo on Wednesday. I give my arm a final shake, and Toby's touch disappears.

I manage to make my body behave until the end of the day. I don't mention the audition to Kat or Bea—it feels wrong to be trying to get into another band when I've only just formed one with Kat. But as I pull open the heavy door to the hall and push my way through velvet curtains, I wish one of them was with me.

The rock music hits me immediately, and so does the sight of Pearl, standing on the stage next to Toby and belting out the words to a song I know but don't particularly like. Pearl can sing and she knows it. Spotting me, she stares at me, and a smile creeps over her face. She seems to be wearing more makeup than ever these days—her eyes are covered in black mascara and eyeliner, and her hair is a tangled mess. Unfortunately, she looks amazing and, of course, she knows it.

I walk toward the stage, my eyes following the long ladder that runs up Pearl's black tights and disappears under her rolled-up skirt. Standing next to Toby, his hair flopping into his eyes as he thrashes his guitar, she looks like she belongs in this band. She looks like she belongs with Toby—two dark angels making a dark noise together . . . oh, and Frank and Dexter from the eleventh grade.

No one else is in the hall. It looks as if Pearl and I are the only ones auditioning. The song finishes and, being the only member of the audience, I feel I have to clap. I don't put much effort into it. "Hi, Sweaty," says Pearl into the microphone. Her words echo around the hall.

So *funny*. Pearl likes to make out that I smell. That's her thing with me. Pearl's got a thing with most girls in our school.

"Is it my turn?" I say, throwing my bag on a chair and standing as tall as my yellow Dr. Martens will let me. *Bring it on, Pearl*, I think as I walk up the stairs at the side of the stage. If I wasn't sure about being in the band when I walked into the hall, now I want it more than anything.

Pearl and I swap places, shrinking away from each other as we pass by Dexter's drum kit. I take my place next to Toby, and she slumps in the front row and gets out her phone.

"Here you go, B-Cakes." Toby smiles and hands me a sheet of lyrics.

I wave it away. "I know them." Even though I don't like the song, I've heard it often enough to pick up the words. I can always do that with songs. Staring straight ahead, I take a deep breath and try to feel soulful and confident. The last time I sang on a stage, I was in the Brownies and I was dressed as a pumpkin . . . and I was rapping.

The band starts. They're shaky, but Toby holds them together. Dexter's passionate drumming thuds through my body, and Toby nods me in. Facing the back of the hall, I start to sing. Pearl's *sweaty* comment burns in my voice, and all I think about is beating her and wiping the smile off her face.

The song stops abruptly, although Dexter can't resist finishing with a series of drum fills. Toby takes the mike off me. "Betty's in," he says, looking down at Pearl. Then, as an afterthought, he adds, "Sorry."

I can't resist it. Looking down at her, I smile and do our Ladybird wave—thumb tucked in and four fingers wiggling. Pearl invented that wave, and we used to do it to each other all day, driving our nursery teacher mad. Pearl stands up, grabs her bag, and strides down the center of the hall, one finger raised behind her back. That's not our Ladybird wave.

She lets the door slam shut after her, and my hand

drops down. My feeling of satisfaction evaporates into the huge, echoing room.

"You totally rocked," says Toby, looking slightly amazed. The rest of Vanilla Chinchilla nods enthusiastically, Frank's red curls bobbing up and down. "Where did that big voice come from?"

"Me!" I say, laughing.

"Well, look after it because our first rehearsal is at my place on Friday."

As Dexter and Frank pack up, Toby walks me off the stage. "We could hang out together afterward," he says, "but only after we've rehearsed. We've got a lot of work to do if we're going to be ready for the concert."

"What?" I pick up my bag, an icy feeling growing in my stomach. "We're doing the Autumn Celebration?"

"That's why we need to rehearse." He leans against the back of a chair and studies me. The icy feeling spreads until I start to feel sick. I know the rules of our school performances: We can perform only once in the evening.

"What's the matter?" Toby glances to the back of the hall, to the door Pearl has just stomped out of.

I have to choose: sing with Kat, or sing with Toby. If I sing with Kat, Pearl gets Toby. I saw them together. I know that's what would happen.

I look up at him. "Nothing," I say with a smile. "Just looking forward to Friday."

As I walk down the central aisle, my stomach churns,

big-time, and part of me seems to drain into the scuffed wooden floor.

Kat is going to kill me.

I walk home in the rain. Black leaves stick to my boots, and the street lamps leave oily reflections on the pavement. A couple of times, I go to call Kat, but I can't do it. I can't think of the words that will make what I've done okay, because it's not okay.

When I get to my road, I turn off my phone and shove it deep in my bag. Then I let myself into a cold house. Dad's not in. He hasn't left a message, and it doesn't feel like he's been back all day. I love it when I get home and hear his music blaring out from the kitchen, the crash of plates as he unloads the dishwasher and the smell of fresh coffee. I can't remember the last time I smelled coffee when I walked in.

The house feels very empty.

It's true when I say I don't miss my mum. How could I? I can't remember anything about her. But sometimes I feel as if something is missing from my life.

Without realizing what I'm doing, I head upstairs and stare at the attic hatch. My heart thuds. What do I think is up there? A ghost Mum sitting on a suitcase, waiting for me to appear? I get the silver pole from the top of Dad's wardrobe and use it to twist the attic hatch open. After clipping the ladder in place, I climb up, the metal icy and damp under my fingers.

Just as I stick my head into the dark space, a *tip tap* makes me turn round. Mr. Smokey has his paws on the bottom rung of the ladder and is staring up at me.

"Go away," I say. "Cats can't climb ladders." But then I realize it would be nice to have him up here, so I go back down, scoop him under my arm, and carry him up.

The dim yellow light reveals paint cans, toys, and overflowing bags piled high in every inch of space. I put Mr. Smokey down, and he disappears in a flash. I go to Mum's corner, treading over Disney Rollerblades and a pile of Dr. Seuss books. The things in Mum's part of the attic are more organized, and each box is labeled with her familiar handwriting. I quickly find what I'm looking for: a pastel blue box with a photo of a lady caressing her silky legs.

I sit on a trunk of Swanette costumes and peer inside the box. At first, all I can see is the electric razor, smooth and white like an egg, but then I spot the familiar lilac envelopes tucked behind the polystyrene packaging. I pull out a handful of letters.

There are four, but they are thick, and each has a different title. There's *The one where I have my first kiss*, *The one where my mum gets a boyfriend*, *The one where I fall in love*, and, at the bottom of the pile, *The one where my heart is broken.*

I guess Mum was a *Friends* fan. I love *Friends*.

Rain falls on the roof, and downstairs I hear the central heating click on. It's so cold up here, I can see my breath. I long to hear Dad's key in the front door, but at the same time I don't want to know that he's been with Poo, and I definitely don't want him to find me up here. Mum's right: This is between her and me.

I hold *The one where my mum gets a boyfriend*, but I don't open it. I'm almost scared about what's inside, and the shadowy attic and howling wind aren't helping.

Suddenly, Mr. Smokey lands on my lap, squashing the letter. I scream and then laugh. "You scared me," I tell him.

I climb down the ladder with Mr. Smokey and the letters. I still have a cold ache inside me when I think about what I've got to tell Kat and the fact that Dad's probably doing a "downward dog" with Poo, but the ache has shrunk from the size of a pineapple to the size of a pear.

"Come on," I say to Mr. Smokey, rubbing my face against his pointy chin. "Let's give Dad a heart attack and unload the dishwasher. I think we can do it in two minutes and beat his personal best."

"Are you joking, Betty?"

Kat stares at me, her blond hair shining in the sun. We're standing outside school at the end of the day.

"I really am sorry, Kat," I say, fiddling with the pompoms on my hat. I force myself to look at her. All around us, students stream out of school, laughing and yelling. "If I don't sing in Toby's band, Pearl will, and you know how much I like him."

"What am I supposed to do?" She shakes her head as she works out what this will mean. "This was going to help me pass my music final . . . I thought you enjoyed rehearsing the other day?"

"I did . . . I loved it!"

"This is Jesus all over again," she says, and this would

be funny if tears weren't spilling out of her eyes. She's being shoved on all sides, but she just stands there, crying and letting herself get pushed around.

"We're still friends, aren't we?" I say, sounding like I'm in the seventh grade.

"*You* are a selfish . . ." She pauses for a moment, then says, "*Moo*!" I want to smile again, but I know she'd never forgive me. "You were selfish when you took Jesus, and you're selfish now!"

Something burns inside me. "What about *you*, Kat?" I say. "Remember when you dumped Bea so you could dance with Pearl in *Starwars*? And then totally ignored her for weeks? That was a pretty *selfish* thing to do."

We stand there staring at each other. "I wouldn't do that now," she says quietly.

"Wouldn't you?"

"No," she says. "Never." Then she pushes past me and joins the stream of students heading away from school.

I walk home, feeling cold and empty. Kat's right; I am being selfish. But I have to sing in Toby's band so I can keep seeing him. Just being near him makes me forget all about Dad and Poo, and I feel like something amazing might happen. I don't know how I can explain this to Kat.

I stop walking. The wind has picked up and leaves are swirling around my feet. My legs are freezing because I'm wearing boots with socks and no tights. Suddenly, I don't want to go home. I'm going to go and see Bill. He always cheers me up.

Soon, I'm building an immense train track with Eric, Bill's brother. Bill's upstairs doing his homework, and his mum says he can't see me until he's finished. I told her it was deadly serious, but she said so were his finals.

"Let's do a massive crash this time," I say as I put in the final piece of track.

"Can we put yogurt on the track?"

"No, your mum told us off the last time we did that. I promised not to do it again." I think for a moment. "How about it crashes into Bubblegum? She's got thick fur and she's quite fat, so it won't hurt her."

"Yes!" says Eric, jumping up and down. "You are *so* cool, Betty."

"No, she's not," says Bill, who's appeared in the doorway. As usual, he's wearing board shorts and a T-shirt. Bill wears shorts for about eleven months of the year. "Betty's *irresponsible*, Eric. There's a difference."

"I am cool," I say. "Don't listen to him."

"Please let us use Bubblegum for the crash!" Eric wraps himself round Bill's leg and sits on his foot. "I won't let go until you say we can." Bill looks down at him and tries to shake him off, but Eric just clings even tighter.

Suddenly, with an Incredible Hulk roar, Bill lifts Eric

up, booming, "Leave my dog alone!" Then he flies him around the room, Eric giggling like crazy, before dropping him on the sofa. "Come on," he says to me, voice back to normal. "Let's go upstairs."

I follow him out. "You find Bubblegum," I whisper to Eric, "and train her to sit on the track."

"I heard that," says Bill from the stairs.

I settle myself on Bill's bed with my feet warming on the radiator. "So the big news is Kat hates me," I say.

"Are you sure you want to tell me about it?" he says. "Isn't that what Bea's for? Can't we just watch *Adventure Time*?"

"No," I say, a lump forming in my throat. "Even cartoons can't make me feel better."

"Even a cartoon with Marceline the Vampire Queen?"

"She said I was a selfish *moo*, Bill!"

"A selfish *moo*?" He laughs. "Wow!"

"I know. Essentially she called me a cow. . . . Didn't she?"

"Yep," says Bill. He flops down on the floor, and I tell him everything that's happened over the past few days, how I'm singing in Toby's band and how I had to tell Kat I was abandoning her.

"Then she *cried* and stormed off," I say, "*and* Dad is forcing me to meet his *lover* tomorrow . . . *and* I want to kiss Toby Gray, but I don't know how to because I've spent all my teenage years hanging out with *you* instead of hanging out with *boys*!"

"First," he says, "I am *actually* a boy. Second, Kat will forgive you eventually, but you'll need to do some massive girlie things to make up for it."

"Like what?"

"Getting her a cuddly toy or making cupcakes."

"That could work," I say, nodding.

"Next, Poo might be the coolest woman on the planet. She might"—Bill looks around his room for inspiration—"read comics, play the banjo, and windsurf."

"You mean she might be a female version of you."

"Exactly."

"What about Toby?" I ask, sitting up. "Can you sort out my love life too?"

"*Adventure Time*?" he asks, reaching for his laptop.

"If you won't help me, maybe I should consult the experts." I pick up a book I've spotted on Bill's bed. "*The Greatest Love Poems of All Time*," I read. "Why've you got this?" I start to flick through it. It's full of highlighted passages. Bill may look like a chilled-out surfer, but he's super clever. He's probably going to get all A's on his finals.

"In the evening," he says, his face serious, "I read love poems and think about *you*, Betty, and how you are as beautiful as the sun and moon and other romantic stuff, and when I find a line that makes me think, that is *so* Betty, I highlight it."

I narrow my eyes. "You're doing it for school, aren't you?"

He smiles. "An English essay."

"Okay, I'll test you." I select one of his highlighted lines. "What does 'She walks in beauty, like the night' mean?"

"Read the next line."

" 'Of cloudless climes and starry skies.' "

"That's by Byron—"

"Correct."

"And he's saying that there are no clouds in the sky, and there are lots of stars. She's as beautiful as a perfect starry night."

"Has she got freckles?"

"You have no soul, Betty."

"No, I like it," I say, getting out my Dennis the Menace sketchbook. "In fact, I'm going to copy it down. I'm going to become an expert on love." When I've finished writing, I shut Dennis.

"Time for cartoons?" Bill asks.

"Time for Epic Silent Dance!" I say. Bill groans, but after a bit more persuading, he finds "50 Epic Dance Moves" on YouTube. "I'm going first," I tell him. "You choose a song for me." I hand him my iPod.

"Today you can Epic Silent Dance to"—Bill fiddles with

the iPod—"this." I press play and "(Your Love Keeps Lifting Me) Higher and Higher" comes on. I warm up with a few hamstring stretches.

"Hit it," I say, and Bill starts the film. Getting totally into the music, I copy the guy in the pink pants who's demonstrating the dance moves. Bill and I have done this so many times, we don't really need the film anymore. Of course, for Bill I'm dancing in silence. He tries hard not to laugh, but he breaks on move five: thrusting. I thrust with my entire body and a lot of enthusiasm.

"Your eyes are sweet, B-Cakes. They're the color of Dove chocolate . . . but better."

I'm in heaven. We're in art, and Toby is drawing my eyes and saying nice things about them.

"Your lashes are massive," he says, peering over his sheet of paper. "But you've got some gunk in the corner of your left eye." Quickly, I wipe it off with my sleeve.

Obviously Kat wouldn't draw anything that belonged to me. She's doing Bea's eyes on the other side of the room and is officially not speaking to me. This has worked out quite well because I got paired with Toby, and right now he's staring deeply into my eyes. Miss Summons actually said, "*Stare* deeply into your partner's eyes." This is my best lesson *ever*, even better than when a drunk Japanese man taught us history and he wasn't even a teacher . . . or supposed to be in the school.

"Don't move," says Toby. "I'm doing the folds of your eyelids."

Hmmm.

"They're like petals . . ."

Better.

". . . on a rose."

Boom!

"My dad's making me meet his new girlfriend tonight," I say.

"You're moving."

"Sorry." I try to freeze my face. "The thing is, I don't want to go. It's just been me and my dad for years."

"My stepfather lets me drive his Range Rover on the hills of the Downs."

"Poo hasn't got a Range Rover. She's got a Fiat."

"Bummer. That won't get you up the hills. You need four-wheel drive."

I think he's missing the point. He makes some bold strokes with his charcoal, then disappears behind his paper. When he reappears, he's drawn a huge, swirling mustache on his own face and written *T-Dog* on his forehead. His face is deadly serious.

"I like it," I say, laughing.

"You're moving again."

"Sorry . . . it's just, it feels weird that my dad has this new best friend who isn't me."

"Forget about it," he says, smiling and making his mustache wiggle. "Think about our rehearsal Friday. We're going to rock, B-Cakes."

I try to forget about it all day, but it's hard to forget about it when I'm walking into Pizza Express and staring straight into Poo's face.

Despite a ridiculously long shower, "losing" one of my Puma trainers, and going back into the house to kiss Mr. Smokey good-bye, Dad has managed to get me here. She's not like I was expecting. Her hair is neat and short, not long and tangled, and she's wearing a polka-dot blouse. There are no beads or flowing skirts, but I do smell a hint of incense when I sit next to her.

"Betty," she says, beaming like she's my number one fan. She has a clean-looking face and pale pink lipstick. Her hands are gripping a napkin and, curiously, each of her nails is painted a different shade of gray. Her little fingernails are painted a deep, sparkling black.

I force my lips into a gesture of a smile. Dad glares at me from behind his menu so I add a small "Hello."

We order our food—*just water for me . . . no doughballs . . . I want a child's pizza . . . no extra pepperoni . . . I don't always have extra pepperoni!* Annoyingly, Dad is set on turning the meal into a celebration.

"Your dad has told me all about you," says Poo as she destroys a bowl of olives. I take a sip of water. "He described how beautifully you've painted your bedroom. I'd love to see it." I take another sip of water. I can't think of anything I could say right now that isn't mean.

"Tell Rue about what you're doing in art at the moment," says Dad. "Rue's an artist. She does amazing woodcut prints."

"Of animals wearing clothes," adds Rue.

I don't tell her what I'm doing in art. Instead I say, "Why are you named Rue?" Dad's eyes suggest I may have used a rude tone, but I honestly can't make my voice any friendlier.

"Well, I'm actually named Tanya. Rue is my middle name. It's a plant."

"It's a stupid name."

Dad breathes in quickly through his nose and opens his mouth, but Rue gets there first. "I know! My dad chose it, and he had bad taste in everything. See?" She puts her hand flat on the table. "Look at this." On her third finger is a ring shaped like a ram with curling horns and swirling wool.

"That's gross," I say.

"Isn't it? But it's the last thing he gave me before he

died, so now I'm stuck with it." She holds it up in front of her face and studies it. "I'd be a total bitch if I didn't wear it."

I nearly smile. It's funny seeing this petite, tidy lady saying that word so sweetly. But there is no way I'm going to laugh. Then Poo starts telling us some story about her dad, and a thought pops into my head. What if she's telling me about her dad so that we'll bond, because we've got something in common, a *dead-parent* thing in common?

"So we're at this wedding, and there was no one dancing," she says, "and the bride was begging people to join her, but no one would." As she talks, she tears a piece of garlic bread into crumbs. "Suddenly, my dad comes back from the bathroom, walks into the middle of the empty dance floor, and starts pogoing like crazy." Rue turns to me. "I was your age, Betty, and I wanted to die of shame, but after a couple of seconds of people staring, openmouthed, everyone got up, and soon the dance floor was heaving!"

She finishes her story, and her face is sparkling with the memory. Dad is gazing at her. They look like me and Toby in art.

"Margherita?" A steaming pizza is put in front of me. I look at it, and I know I'm going to cry. I don't even think I can get to the bathroom before Dad and Rue notice.

"Pogoing looks like this," says Dad, and he starts jerking his head up and down like a chicken.

"Black pepper?" the waitress asks, looking at Dad out of the corner of her eye.

I ignore her and turn to Poo. "Are you saying that we have something in common because your dad is dead and so is my mum?"

"Betty," says Dad, "watch it."

"Because we have *nothing* in common. You have a *stupid* name, *horrible* jewelry and"—I pause and look up at Dad's horrified face, but nothing can stop me now—"an *embarrassing* dad."

"Betty," she says, pointing at the Pingu necklace around my neck and then looking at Dad, whose hair is still sticking up from the pogoing, "I think we might have a little bit in common." She's not embarrassed or even annoyed.

That's it. A tear rolls down my cheek. I get up, grab my coat, and run out of the restaurant.

Dad catches up with me at the end of the road and pulls me round by my shoulder.

We stare at each other in silence. I'm shaking and so is Dad. His mouth is a tight line. "Right now, I don't like you very much, Betty," he says. Then he turns and walks back to the restaurant.

It's the worst thing he has ever said to me. It's the worst thing anyone has ever said to me. I walk home, wiping the tears off my face.

I hope Dad will jump in the car and try to catch up with

me so he can say sorry, but he doesn't. When I walk into our house, I know he's chosen Poo and a pizza over me. Mr. Smokey must be out terrorizing small mammals. I'm totally alone.

I flop facedown on my bed and let a wave of anger sweep through me. I think about ringing Bill or Bea, but instead I pull the Puma box out from under my bed and take out Mum's letters. I shuffle through them until I find the one I'm looking for: *The one where my mum gets a boyfriend.* Pulling the duvet around me, I rip open the envelope, pull out three sheets of paper, and start to read.

Dear Plumface,
At some point, Dad will get a new girlfriend. This is fine, and the thought isn't making me feel very, very sick at all. If he meets her when you're little, you might not even realize she is a new girlfriend, and you will grow up calling her Mum.

That hurts.

I think I'm going to focus on what's happening right now and the past. When I think about the future, I find it hard to breathe. What's happening right now is that you've gone to the park with Dad so I can pack for the hospital. The doctors have decided I've got to go back in because I'm not doing so well at the moment. Actually, let's just focus on the past.

Here's the story about when your nanna got a

boyfriend. I was thirteen, Auntie Kate was eight, and Nanna's "special friend" was a policeman. The first time I met him, he picked us up in his red van and took us to the seaside. I wore a T-shirt that had Happy Days *written over a rainbow. I was wearing it to be sarcastic, but nobody got it. Plus it was so cold, I had to do up the zip on my fake suede jacket.*

Auntie Kate was a very lovable child, and amazingly this affection that she felt for everyone and everything even extended to Nanna's policeman, who giggled *and had long white hairs curling out of his eyebrows. The more Auntie Kate romped with him—skimming stones, running away from waves, drawing faces in patches of sand—the crosser I got. Mum (aka your nanna) sat next to me on the pebbles and kept saying things like, "He's great with her, don't you think?" and "Just listen to those two!"*

I had no choice. Their high-pitched giggles were being lifted high on the sea breeze and slammed into my face, repeatedly. Kate was such a traitor.

"Isn't this a beautiful day?" said Mum, nudging me and licking her strawberry ice cream in an infuriating way.

"No," I said. "It's a @$#! day." Betty, I have to confess that I swore *at Nanna. Now you probably see her as a sweet lady who wears colorful beads, does crosswords, and makes the best roasted potatoes. Back then, on that*

windy beach, she was a deeply annoying lady who was lusting over a man with badger eyebrows. Have I mentioned that all afternoon he called me Laura *and not* Lorna?

Mum sucked in her breath and looked stupid because she had an ice cream mustache, and then I said, "The only good thing about today is this.*" I pointed at a rock I had just noticed. It must have been a bit of wall once because you could see all the different colored bricks arranged in lines. It was a very big rock. "I'm going to take it home," I said.*

And I nearly did. I hauled it up the beach, along the walkway, and put it by Mum's feet in the van. Unfortunately, when we were halfway home, I said the policeman's Christmas tree air freshener smelled of vomit (it didn't), so Mum opened her door and rolled my rock out into the gutter.

"Stop the van!" I screamed at the policeman, but Mum refused to let him. All the way home I sobbed, "I want my rock. . . . I want my rock!"

Did I mention I was thirteen?

The minute we got home, I leaped out of the van and walked back the way we had come. Eventually, I found my rock and carried it home. It took me three hours. I lugged the rock up to my bedroom and kept it there until I went to college.

After the trip to the beach with the policeman,

Nanna made us go on days out with quite a few boyfriends—actually, to be fair, there were only three—but only one of them stuck around: your gramps. The day I left for college, he carried my rock down the stairs and packed it carefully between my boxes in the back of his van. When we were on the highway, he said, "Look in the glove box. I've made you a present."

I pulled out a cassette. Gramps had made me a compilation of music. On the insert, in tiny capital letters, he'd written the names of all the songs he'd chosen. He'd used three different colored pens, red, green, and black. "They're all female singers, like you," he said as I put the cassette into the stereo.

A truck thundered past just as the opening track started. First I heard a guitar, crackly and distant, and then a woman's voice singing, "Kiss me each morning, for a million years."

"That's Bettye Swann," said Gramps. "She's my favorite." Each word she sang felt like breath whispered on my neck. Then Gramps started tapping the steering wheel really hard because the track was a bit soppy and he was embarrassed.

Hearing that Bettye Swann song led to my obsession with all things connected to the sixties, including my band, the Swanettes. The Swanettes led me to the pub where I met your dad. If you think about it, if Gramps had never made me that tape, Dad and I would never have made you (sorry, traumatic thought, but true).

Did you know that Gramps used to be a policeman? I bet his eyebrows are like woolly mammoths by now.

Love you always,

Mumface xx

I read the letter three times, then I put it back in its purple envelope. Gramps's eyebrows would be like woolly mammoths if Nanna didn't trim them once a week during *Antiques Roadshow*.

Pulling myself out of bed, I trudge downstairs. I have that tired feeling all through my body that comes from crying too much.

I get myself some Mini-Wheats and eat my cereal staring at the messages Dad and I have written all over the fridge: *pUt chip5 iN oven, luv YA bumface, betty5 the bomb*. We lost all the *s* magnets a long time ago.

Before I go to bed, I sweep a clear circle in the center of the fridge door and write: *5orry dAd.*

8.

"Sadder," says Toby. I lower my voice and slow down. "A little sadder."

I'm in Toby's garage being taught how to "sing miserable." The garage is bigger than the entire downstairs of my house and has a carpet, lights, and heating. It isn't even joined to his house but is in a separate part of the yard. The other half of Vanilla Chinchilla, Dexter and Frank, are "taking five" while Toby and I sit on an old sofa and go through the song we're singing for the Autumn Celebration. Toby's written it and it's called "Shut Up!"

"Basically, Betty," he says, "I want it to sound grungy, so you need to sound flatter when you sing." We're facing each other, and our knees are touching. Dexter is teaching Frank how to drum roll, and the constant drumming combined with the knee contact is making my mind buzz.

I try the opening verse again. Toby watches me with narrowed eyes. "Better," he says, "but it could still sound cooler."

This time, I drain all the emotion out of my voice. I sound so dull I almost laugh, but Toby nods and I know I'm getting it right. When I finish, he leans back and studies me for a moment, and then he smiles and says, "Perfect."

We run through "Shut Up!" several times, and it's starting to sound okay. Even though Toby's younger than Dexter and Frank, it's clear Vanilla Chinchilla is his band. He's constantly telling us to speed up, slow down, get louder or quieter. Usually, he's right. We call it a day when Dexter's mum calls and says she's waiting for him outside.

As Dexter and Frank pack up the drum kit, I stick around, wondering what to do. After all, wasn't there a promise of "hanging out"? I'd love to go explore Toby's house. I caught a glimpse of it on my way in, and it's huge, all black and white like a building from Shakespeare's time, with three pointy roofs.

"Betty, Betty, Betty," sings Toby from the sofa as he strums away on his guitar. He grins and beckons me over. "Betty, Betty, Betty," he repeats as I sit down opposite him, "feelin' sweaty, sweaty, sweaty in the Serengeti eatin' hot spaghetti!"

Not quite the love song I was hoping for, but I could sit and watch him play the guitar for hours.

"See you later," calls Frank from the door. Toby stops

playing and puts his guitar on the floor. There is this delicious moment, when it's finally just the two of us, and Toby is staring at me and I'm thinking, is this *it* . . . ? Are we going to kiss? Am I finally going to get to use my apple skills? Okay, I admit it, I tried Kat's apple suggestion. It was both funny and nutritious but not very helpful kissing practice. Toby smiles and I start to blush. I just can't help it, and this makes him smile even more.

"Hey," he says. "Can you come to Brighton next Saturday?"

I look at him to check he's serious. "Sure," I say, like it's the kind of thing boys are always asking me to do. Inside, my mind is running through all the possibilities of what this might mean and words like *date* and *girlfriend* keep popping up.

"You can meet my friends from my old school." Promising . . . very promising. "They'll like you. You're cool. . . ." Then he reaches toward me, cups my chin in one hand, and says, "Very cool." My cheeks are burning so much he probably needs to run his hand under cold water for ten minutes.

"Thanks," I say in a slightly squeaky way because my cheeks are pressed together.

"No worries." Toby lightly slaps my blushing cheek and jumps up off the sofa. "Right, I'm kinda busy now, so . . ."

"Oh, okay." I start to gather my things together, pulling

on my hat. Obviously there's been a change of plan. Toby waits by the garage door for me, one hand on the light switch. "See you later, alligator," I say, for some terrible reason.

"Sure thing, B-Cakes." Suddenly we're standing very close. I look up at him and he grins, revealing his perfect white teeth, but he doesn't move. I duck down under his arm and squeeze past him, brushing against his warm chest. He follows me out, locking the door. Then, after a final wave, we head off in separate directions, our feet crunching on the gravel.

I wander home, my mind buzzing with questions, and without really realizing it I take a detour and head toward Bill's. It's starting to get dark, but people haven't shut their curtains yet. I peer into each house in turn—I love doing this—studying the lit-up rooms. Tonight I keep spotting mums. One's bending over a sink, her arms plunged in bubbly water. Another is flopped on a sofa with a cup of tea resting on her tummy, and then I see one on her hands and knees picking up toys. I think they're mums because there are messes all around them.

I find Bill in his garage, which is different from Toby's because it is actually a garage, with old bikes and tools, a lightbulb hanging from the ceiling, and lots of cobwebs. Really this is Bill's garage—his mum gave up on it years ago—and the back wall is taken up with the rack he built to store his windsurfing kit.

"Hello," he says, glancing up from the board he's mending. I sit on a stool and watch as he presses pink putty into a hole and starts to sand it down. It's relaxing, a bit like watching Kat put on her makeup. The garage is warm. There's an electric heater next to me with three bars glowing hot and orange. Bill blows dust from the top of the board. "So what's up?" he asks, wiping the board clean with a cloth.

"Nothing," I say. Eric's left some Lego men sitting on the table. There's Batman carrying a chicken leg and Yoda from *Star Wars*. For some reason, Yoda's wearing a lady's skirt. I pick him up and walk him toward Batman.

"Know not if I have a boyfriend, do I, Batman," I say, in my best Yoda voice.

Bill shakes his head and picks up Batman. "Yoda," he says, his voice a deep growl, "your impression is shocking. You sound Welsh."

"If Toby-Wan Kenobi asks me to go to Brighton on Saturday," carries on Yoda, undeterred, "a date it is?"

"Perhaps, Yoda." Bill makes Batman fly up to Yoda's face. Batman starts to hit Yoda with the chicken leg. "Do you want to go to Brighton with this Toby?"

"Exciting it will be."

"I will be walking among you in Brighton on Saturday," snarls Batman, "watching Bea and Ollie jive at the Churchill Square shopping center . . . and fighting evil."

"What?" I say, abandoning Yoda.

"Check your phone," says Bill. "You're invited, too."

"That is *so* weird," I say, pulling out my phone. Sure enough, there's Bea's text saying we should all go to Brighton together. "What are you doing hanging out with my friends?" I say. "I guess Bea's trying to get us together so that me and Kat can make up."

"There's no wind forecast for Saturday, so I said I'd go." He shrugs, not seeing what the big deal is. He's hung out with my friends before, but I've always been there. "Obviously, I thought you'd be coming, too."

"I've already said I'll go to Brighton with Toby. Maybe we can all meet up?" I try to imagine it in my head.

"Okay," says Bill.

I help him pack up because I don't really want to leave the warmth of the garage and go home. What if Poo is sitting on my sofa with a cup of tea on her stomach? "How's your love thingy going?" I ask Bill as we lift his board back onto the rack.

"Not so well," he says.

"You know it'll be fine. You get perfect marks in everything."

"Not everything," he says. He opens the garage door, and a gust of wind swooshes through the gap, bringing in a pile of dead leaves.

"Give me a line of poetry for the road," I say. "I liked the starry skies one."

He looks at me and thinks for a moment. "Here's one

from a play," he says. " 'Love is like a child that longs for every thing it can come by.' "

I duck down under the half-open door and repeat it a couple of times in my head. "So who said it, and what does it mean?"

"William, or, as I prefer to call him, *Bill* Shakespeare said it, and it means that if you're in love, you're happy with any tiny bit of attention you get from the person you love . . . just like children think everything is amazing." I must look confused because he adds, "Remember Eric when I gave him that cardboard box? It was just an old box, but he turned it into a prison for his Moshi Monsters and played with it for hours."

"I think I get it," I say, remembering the times I hovered outside Toby's classroom waiting for him to come out and maybe, just maybe, say a few words to me. Then I grin. "I don't want to scare you or anything, Bill, but I think Kat might be *longing* for a bit of you."

"What?"

"Seriously. She said you were *cutesome*."

Bill rolls his eyes. "She did not," he says. Then, for the second time today, a boy shuts me out of his garage.

I think about love all the way home. More specifically, I think about whether I'm *in* love with Toby Gray all the way home.

As soon as I get in, I head upstairs because I've got a plan. I'm going to analyze the evidence and work out exactly what's going on with me and Toby. I open up my Dennis the Menace book and find a blank page. Dennis is going to become my Big Book of Love. First I write down Bill's quote—*Love is like a child that longs for every thing it can come by*—then I draw a love grid.

YES, I AM DEFINITELY IN LOVE WITH TOBY.	NO, I'M IN SOMETHING WITH TOBY, BUT IT MIGHT NOT BE LOVE.
His touch makes me feel funny in my tummy . . . and my arms, legs, fingers, hair follicles, eyeballs, and generally everywhere.	The funny feeling in my tummy isn't entirely good. Sometimes it's a bit like the time that big dog barked in my face in the park (i.e., scary).
I know where he is the second he walks into a room, like he's the North Pole and I'm a big magnet.	Sometimes he makes me stop being Betty-ish. For example, this morning, I wanted to wear my Hello Kitty crocheted hat, which essentially gives me a kitten's head, but I didn't because last time I wore it he said I looked like a giant baby.
I love being near him, just like Eric loves mud, rain, stones, buttons, and empty boxes.	I'm not sure he walks in beauty like the night. It's more like he walks in hotness like a panther.

So that didn't help.

I can't call Kat, Bill's already given me his Shakespeare advice, so that leaves Bea . . . or Dead Mum. Bea doesn't answer her phone, so I have to go with Dead Mum. I know which letter I want to read: *The one where I fall in love*.

I don't want to open the letter if there's a chance Dad could walk in. I haven't told him about the letters, and I'm enjoying having a secret from him. I decide that the safest place is in the bath.

Ten minutes later, I'm up to my nose in Wolfberry bubbles (gift from Poo to my dad—I use half the bottle), and the door is locked. After carefully wiping my hands on a towel, I open *The one where I fall in love* and pull out two crisp sheets of paper. Three papery petals fall into the bath. I sink down into the bubbles, keeping my hands up high, and start to read.

Dear Plumface,
Being in love can be very confusing, especially the first time you experience it. It's a bit like the London Underground.

The first time I fell in love was with Rich, and I was eleven years old. Every break time for a week, Rich gave me a Curly Wurly. Just in case Curly Wurlies don't exist anymore and you're thinking I was getting an exotic love bite, don't worry, a Curly Wurly is a twisty bar of toffee covered in chocolate. If I'm honest, back then they were just about the cheapest chocolate you could buy, but it was still enough to make me hold Rich's clammy hand under the desk and to scratch "I love Rich Musher" on the lid of my Ghostbusters pencil tin.

With the benefit of hindsight, I wasn't actually in love with Rich; I just really liked Curly Wurlies. I am so glad I didn't marry him, Betty. Imagine it, Lorna Musher.

The first time I really *fell in love, I was fifteen and it was with Carlo Ferrari.* Lorna Ferrari . . . *now that's more like it! Carlo moved to our school from Wales. The moment he walked into my classroom, I fell for him big time. He had these huge brown eyes that made my internal organs dissolve, and just looking at his fingers made me blush because I wanted them to touch me so badly. Not in a rude way, just in a holding-hands, pushing-a-strand-of-my-hair-behind-my-ear type of way. Best of all, he was brave.*

There was this girl in our class called Eleanor who had acne. Every single day, when she walked into our homeroom, a boy called Jamie Watts called her Pizza-Face. The rest of us just watched this happening because we were so relieved Jamie wasn't calling us Pizza-Face. On Carlo's first day, he heard Jamie doing his pizza-face routine, and he walked right up to him, stared into his eyes, pointed a finger at him, and said, "Shut it, boy!" (Remember, he came from Wales.) Jamie never called Eleanor names again.

When Carlo became one of my best friends, I still loved him. When he started going out with Eleanor a year later, I still loved him. When I went to college, I still loved him. I never told anyone that I was in love with Carlo Ferrari . . . until now.

These petals are from a rose he gave me. A while after he stood up to Jamie, we were walking home from school when he disappeared into someone's garden and then reappeared holding the most beautiful pink rose I had ever seen. He handed it to me, and there was this amazing moment when the world stood still and I knew I was seconds away from discovering what it felt like to hold Carlo's wonderful hand. Then I said, "Thanks," and I shoved the rose in my bag like he'd just given me a Curly Wurly. I was so in love with Carlo, I couldn't believe he would like me . . . even when he gave me a rose. A rose, *Betty! The international symbol for* I love you. *Two weeks later, he started going out with Eleanor.*

I was way *funnier than Eleanor. I would have been a great girlfriend for Carlo.*

But who is this waiting just round the corner . . . ? It's Nick Plum: painter-decorator, lover of soul music, and the bravest man on the planet . . . oh, and your dad, of course. Now, that was love, all right, but it's a whole different story.

I'm not sure who you'll fall in love with or when it

will happen. Right now you are in love with me and your dad, so you're in safe hands.

Reading over this letter it all seems to make sense, but at the time, when Rich said he wouldn't give me any more Curly Wurlies unless I kissed him, and when I saw Carlo and Eleanor holding hands, I felt totally lost. If you feel lost when you fall in love, stay where you are, don't panic, and think. Just like you would if you were lost on the London Underground. I'm sure you'll find your way home.

Love you always,
Mumface xxx

I put the letter on the edge of the sink and try to scoop the rose petals out of the water, but they disintegrate into nothing. My bath's gone cold, so I turn on the hot tap with my toe and sink under the churning water. Thanks for that, Mum: *Stay where you are, don't panic, and think.* Worst advice ever. But then again, what did I expect? I chose *The one where I fall in love* because I hoped she'd somehow help me understand what's going on with Toby. But how could she have predicted that I'd fall in love with a supernaturally hot boy who would invite me to Brighton and then throw me out of his garage?

It looks like I'm going to have to work this one out on my own.

9.

"Mint, Betty?" With one hand on the wheel, Toby's mum turns round and waves a packet of Life Savers in my direction.

"I'm fine, thanks," I say. Really, I'd like her to concentrate on the road. Toby and I were supposed to get the bus to Brighton, but as I was waiting outside Aldi, a blue sports car roared up and Toby stuck his head out of the window and told me to jump in. Now I'm sunk down low in a black leather seat listening to R. Kelly.

Every now and then, Toby's mum's eyes flick up to the rearview mirror, checking me out, and I smile and try to look nice and friendly. I don't think she's that impressed. From studying her eyes, I can see they are perfectly made up, and each of her lashes is curved and defined. I rummage in my bag to find a way of improving myself and pull out a tin of cocoa butter Vaseline. I take off my black-rimmed specs—I don't need them, but I think they make me look clever—put them in my bag, and then run my fingers through my hair.

"Are you two okay to make your own way home?" she shouts over the music. I nod and smile a glossy smile. "It's just I'm staying over in Brighton tonight." I smile again. Suddenly, Toby turns up the music and, in perfect synchrony, they both start singing "Sex Me."

"Mum's a big R. Kelly fan," says Toby as the track ends, and I see her eyes flick up to the mirror.

I smile enthusiastically and desperately try to remember the name of an R. Kelly track. "I love 'Black Panties'!" I yell, very pleased with myself. Her eyes widen and then flick back to the road as I'm drowned out by the next track.

I decide to shut up and look out the window. I'm feeling a bit guilty sitting here zooming along the fast lane toward Brighton. When Dad asked what I was doing today, I said *we* were going to go to Brighton, knowing he'd assume that "we" was some combination of Bea, Kat, and Bill.

It's only since I've been a sophomore that Dad's let me go to Brighton with my friends, and there's no way he'd let me go with Toby, because he doesn't even know he exists. He knows I'm performing in the Autumn Celebration, but that's it. Luckily he's too distracted by his love affair with Poo to notice my world's been turned upside down.

I've kept a record of this week's Toby-love in Dennis:

1. Monday, he gave me the bigger half of his Snickers.
2. Wednesday—rehearsal—he looked at me while I was singing, then looked away quite quickly.
3. Thursday, he called me "the T-Dog's one and only B-Cakes" in front of Kat, and after rehearsal he held my finger (okay, he kind of grabbed it to stop me touching his new guitar, but he didn't have to keep hold of it for as long as he did).
4. Friday, he said Saturday would be "wicked hanging with his mates and the B-Cakes."

"Friends" turns out to be "friend," and his name is Nat. We meet him in the Lanes, and Toby does a complicated handshake-punching thing with him before saying, "This is Betty," and nodding in my direction.

"Hi," I say, giving a wave. Nat is like a blond version of Toby. They're both wearing low-slung skinny jeans, T-shirts, and Diesel jackets. And they're both tall. Standing next to them, in my panda hat, cutoffs, and DMs, I feel like their scruffy little sister.

"All right," says Nat, then grabs Toby round the neck and rubs his knuckles into his scalp. "I missed you, T-Dog!"

"C'mon," says Toby, shaking him off, "I need some sneakers."

We spend the next hour wandering around looking for the perfect pair of sneakers for Toby. I love shopping in Brighton, and Bill and I come whenever he's not windsurfing and one of us has some money. We always do the same thing: go to Dave's Comics (best comic shop in the world), drift around the secondhand shops and find funny objects, go and play with Legos in the Lego shop, and then buy a doughnut from the Mock Turtle. They're massive—the size of a baby's face.

Today, we walk straight past Dave's Comics, but I don't mind. I'm just happy being seen next to Toby. At one point, as we cross the road, I catch our reflection in a shop window. In slo-mo, I see him drop his arm across my shoulders and leave it there for a couple of seconds. I get double electric shocks because I see it happen before I feel it. My reflection grins, and I look like one happy panda.

It's only when I glance at my phone and realize it's twelve that I start to worry about missing Bollie's dance. It was supposed to start at midday. I find Toby by the high-tops. "Can we go to Churchill Square now?" I ask.

"Betty's friends are dancing there," Toby tells Nat. "They do, like, ballroom." He starts walking up and down the shop in a pair of gray Nikes. They're really expensive, but his mum gave him a little wad of cash as we got out of the car, so I guess he can afford them. "Nat, do I look like a douche?"

"Nah, man," says Nat.

"It's jive," I tell Nat. "And some of my friends are going to watch. I said I'd meet them there."

"Sure," says Nat. "Burger King's that way."

"I'm just gonna try these in blue," says Toby. I glance at my phone. I've got a message from Bill: **They're on . . . where are you?**

"Can I meet you there?" Suddenly I really want to see my friends, particularly as I know they're only a few minutes away.

"Chillax, B-Cakes. We'll see you there in five."

"Don't miss it," I say as I head for the door. "They're really good."

"Five minutes," he says, taking a pair of Vans off the shelf.

I book it up the hill and hear the music before I see the crowd. There are so many people I can't see any dancers, so I squeeze my way to the front and just manage to catch the last minute of Bea and Ollie's dance. Bea is wearing a red polka-dot dress. I can't take my eyes off her as she bounces, spins, and twirls. Neither can the audience. Ollie's clearly the perfect partner because everything he does just shows off Bea's amazing dancing. They finish with Bea rolling over Ollie's back and popping back up through his legs. Then the applause starts, and Bea's in Ollie's arms, eyes shining.

The music starts again, and they join the other dancers, going round the audience and encouraging everyone to join in.

That's when I spot Bill and Kat. They're sitting on a low wall, the sun shining on their blond heads. Kat's saying something to Bill, and I see his serious face break into a smile. Then she gets up and heads into the middle of the crowd, doing a little dance all on her own. Kat doesn't usually like to stand out, and I can tell from her face that she's desperately hoping Bill will join her. And Bill is so nice that he does. Shaking his head, he goes to her and they hold hands, and they do the most hopeless jive I've ever seen. Their feet are all over the place, and they keep missing each other's hands and bumping into the people around them. They can't stop laughing.

Slowly, I back away. I can't push my way through all the dancers, tap Bill and Kat on the shoulder, and say, "Stop having fun—I'm here!" Especially as Kat probably still hates me. Where is Toby? I glance around the crowd, then check my phone. He's sent me a message: **Find us in b-king b-cakes i got you a whopper xx t**

He isn't coming. Amazingly, the two kisses quickly dissolve my disappointment. I wanted my friends to properly meet Toby, but it looks like they're getting along fine without me.

I take one last look at Bill and Kat. In a matter of minutes they've got the hang of the dance, and now they don't look so ridiculous. In fact, they look quite good. I thought Kat was playing around when she said Bill was cutesome, but, watching them together, I'm not so sure. Kat's perfect hair is getting tangled as she turns round, and her cheeks are bright red, and Bill . . . he looks different, somehow.

I turn away and walk toward Burger King. I text Bill:

Couldn't see you guys in crowd x Betty

Toby and Nat are sitting at a corner table. When I see that Toby has drawn a ketchup heart on the top of my Whopper, my heart lifts. I look at him, and he winks as I slip in next to him on the bench.

"You owe Nat money," says Toby.

"Right." I tear my eyes away from him and get out my purse. I pass Nat a five, and he shoves it in his pocket. Suddenly, I feel Toby's leg rest, ever so slightly, against mine. Even though I'm surrounded by screaming children and the air is thick with the smell of fries, I feel the yummy glow creep over me. Who would have thought Burger King could feel so explosive?

"Do you like the picture I did?" Toby asks. I nod and nibble a french fry. "It's Nat's ass!" he says, grinning.

"Oh." I turn my burger round. "I see it now," I say. Toby winks at me and takes a huge bite out of his Double Whopper.

After hanging around the shops for a bit longer, we head down to the seafront and walk toward the marina. The blue sky has been hidden by clouds, and it's turning wild. We pull our hoods up and battle against the wind, yelling when spray from the sea hits our faces. I don't realize we're heading anywhere in particular until Nat says to Toby, "In there?" and nods toward a peeling Victorian shelter.

It's good to be out of the cold, but it's dark and dirty in the shelter. Flyers and takeout cartons blow around the floor. Also, it smells of wee. Nat and Toby go to the back, but I stay where I am. I'd rather be near fresh air. Suddenly, my phone beeps. It's a message from Bea: **Hey sorry we missed you we're going on the crazy mouse wahoooo!!!! Wanna come??? Xx**

Bea loves the Crazy Mouse. It's this roller coaster at the end of the pier. I look across the sea. The pier's covered in twinkling lights that are reflecting in the churning sea. Right at the end, I can just see the twisting track of the Crazy Mouse. I glance back into the shadows of the shelter, where Toby and Nat are sitting on a rusting bench. Drink cartons and tissues are stuffed down its slats. **Have fun . . . I can almost see you xx** I text back.

Nat opens his backpack and pulls out different cans, carefully lining them up.

"What are you doing?" I ask.

"This, Betty," Toby says, opening a can and giving it a shake, "is a bit more of my bad stuff." Then he jumps up on the bench and, with a swoop of his arm and a hiss from the can, starts to spray an enormous *T* on the wooden wall of the shelter. I glance over my shoulder, but the sidewalk is deserted. Nat stands next to Toby and starts on his own graffiti. From what I can make out, he's spraying the outline of a green furry fish. A gust of wind slips into the shelter, and I pull my hood tight round my face.

"I tagged our school's chapel, and they freaked out," says Toby. "Apparently I ruined a nineteenth-century panel."

"Isn't what you're doing illegal?" I ask.

"All right, Mum," says Nat, laughing.

"Graffiti is illegal," says Toby turning the *o* in *T-Dog* into a snarling bulldog. "But what we're doing is *art*. Like Banksy."

I'm not so sure. What they're doing looks pretty much exactly like graffiti. I turn back toward the boardwalk. Someone's got to be their lookout, and if I don't watch I can pretend they're not doing it. The rain clouds make it seem later than it is, and the pier glitters in the darkness. If I stare hard enough, I can just about see a carriage slowly climbing the track of the Crazy Mouse. Are they all on there right now? It hovers for a second at the top before zooming down. I imagine their screams. I guess Kat is sitting with Bill. He loves fast rides and roars all the way through the scary parts.

"Hey, B-Cakes, what d'you think?" Toby is standing next to his graffiti. Honestly? It's a bit messy and drippy, and the shading's gone wrong. Still, his is definitely better than Nat's.

"It's good," I say. Then, because Toby's waiting for more, I add, "It's massive." I mean it's big—it stretches across the whole of the back wall of the shelter—but Toby thinks I mean massively awesome. He grins as he jumps off the bench.

After he's put the finishing touches to his furry fish (which is actually a wolf), Nat heads home. Before Toby and I leave, he gets out his phone and takes a photo of his art. Suddenly, it feels extra quiet in the shelter, and even the crash of the sea dies away. We're standing so close together, our shoulders are touching. This feeling creeps through me that Toby might do or say something.

But the shelter still smells like pee, and the pier looks so pretty that I don't want to be in here a minute longer.

"C'mon," I say, stepping out onto the boardwalk. "Let's go." Immediately, sea spray mists my face and a gust of wind tugs me forward. Toby joins me, and we run laughing toward town, being knocked on all sides by the wind.

As the bus sways back across the Downs, Toby drops a crumpled Burger King bag on my lap.

"What's that?" I ask.

"A present," he says. "You said you liked it."

I open the bag and pull out a necklace. It's a curled-up fox made out of a thin disc of wood hanging on a chain. Foxes are my favorite animal. Earlier we walked past a stall where a man was making them, and I pointed the necklace out to Toby.

After putting it on, I study the tiny carved lines of its nose and ears. Buying me a necklace . . . this tells me Toby likes me, doesn't it? There's just one problem. I didn't actually see Toby buy it. Did he run back and get it when I went up to watch Bea dance? There definitely would have been time. Also, why would you steal something if you had a pocketful of money? I tuck the necklace inside my coat.

"I love it," I say.

10.

It's almost dark when I get to my road, and I see my house lit up and looking all cozy. Toby and I said good-bye at the bus stop because he had to go round to Dexter's and watch *Bad Asses*. Apparently it's the sequel to *Bad Ass*. I've remembered word for word our good-bye so I can write it in Dennis the minute I get in:

Toby: *See you.*

Me: *Thanks for my fox.*

Toby: *Now you'll never forget our first trip to Brighton.* (Little wave from me, gorgeous eyebrow wriggle from him.)

First trip to Brighton!

I'm actually smiling when I let myself in, but that vanishes when I hear two voices coming from the kitchen. One of them is definitely female and has a Poo-ish quality. I'm just about to sneak upstairs when Dad sticks his head out.

"There you are!" he says, holding the door wide open. I'm still considering running to my room, but then I notice he's made caramel slices and, honestly, I would put up with anyone's company for one bite of Dad's famous caramel slices.

They're piled up high on a plate in front of Poo. The shortbread is golden brown, the caramel is oozy, and they're smothered in thick cracked chocolate. It's as though Dad has set a Betty trap to lure me into the kitchen.

I sit down on the edge of a chair and pick up a caramel slice. "Hi," I say, trying my absolute hardest to be nice . . . or at least not to be nasty.

"Did you get anything in Brighton?" Poo asks. She's sitting cross-legged on one of our kitchen chairs and sipping herbal tea. Either she brought her own tea bag or Dad's got them for her.

"This," I say, holding out my fox necklace.

"Beautiful," she says, leaning forward and picking up the necklace. She runs her fingers over the lines of the fox's face. Today her nails are painted various shades of orange, although everything else about her is totally boring. She's wearing a blue top, jeans, and, just like last time, her hair is short and shiny.

I look over at my dad in his almost skinny jeans and faded green T-shirt that says I ♥ BEARDS. He looks cool. I like having a cool-looking dad. Poo just doesn't suit him.

"Foxes are my favorite animal," she says, letting go of my necklace.

"Really?" I say. *As if!* Rue would say anything to make me like her. I narrow my eyes as Dad puts a cup of tea in front of me.

"Absolutely," she says. "In fact, I've a tattoo of a fox on my arm." And just as I'm thinking she's probably got some lame cartoon fox on her wrist, she rolls up her sleeve and shows me her tattoo. That's definitely a fox. It's all done in black ink, its pointy nose touching her hand and its tail curving into her elbow. Poo's got a whopping big fox running up her arm.

"Wow," I say, before I can stop myself, which is so annoying because immediately I sense how pleased Dad is. Quickly, I add, "I prefer owls."

"I've got an owl on my shoulder," she says.

What? I bet if I said I liked zedonks, she'd show me one on her bum. We've definitely done enough bonding. Balancing one more caramel slice on the top of my mug, I stand up. On the way out of the kitchen, Dad gives me the most grateful smile I've ever seen, and all for saying *this*, *really*, *wow*, and *I prefer owls*.

Upstairs, I write in Dennis and check my phone. I've got a message from Bill: **Crazy Mouse + doughnut = good**.

They all got a Mock Turtle doughnut! How can I be

jealous of a doughnut? It's like they had my best day out ever and didn't invite me . . . although they did invite me, of course. I force myself to think of Toby and me on the bus, knocking into each other when we went around corners, and how he smelled of this yummy mix of fabric softener, spray paint, and Toby. The bus journey took half an hour. The Crazy Mouse probably lasted only a couple of minutes. But I do love doughnuts. . . .

Just as I'm feeling all my good Toby-vibes slipping away from me, the doorbell rings. I hear Dad open the door and then a muffled voice. It's Bill! I launch myself off the bed and into the hallway.

"Hi," I yell, jumping down the stairs two at a time. Bill can't let Dad know that I wasn't in Brighton with him!

"Haven't you had enough of her?" Dad says as Bill steps into the house.

"Clearly he hasn't," I say, landing in front of them with a bang. "Bill, you loser, stop stalking me." Bill looks confused for a second, then picks up on my wide, pleading eyes. "We've only just said good-bye," I add pointedly.

"Yeah, I know," says Bill, "but you forgot your doughnut, so we thought we'd bring it around." He holds out a paper bag. *We?* And then I see Kat hovering behind him.

"My favorite," I say, pulling it out of the bag and taking a big bite.

"Two caramel slices not enough for you?" asks Dad.

"Nope," I say, licking up the dripping jam. "Coming up to my room?" I really need to get them away from Dad. As they follow me up the stairs, I notice Poo standing in the kitchen doorway.

"Hi," she says, taking a sip of her tea, her eyes looking at me over the rim. She knows. Somehow she worked out what my dozy dad couldn't see.

"Bill, Kat, this is . . ." I hesitate for a second before forcing myself to say, "Rue." Then I whisk them up to the safety of my bedroom.

As soon as the door shuts, Bill starts setting up my Nintendo. It's ancient, probably an antique. My mum got it for my dad to celebrate their first wedding anniversary. This time he connects three controllers.

"Hey," I say to Kat, who's hovering by the door. "I really am sorry about the Autumn Celebration—"

"Shh!" she says, putting a finger to her lips. Then she smiles. "Bill told me how heartbroken you've been and how you were planning to make cupcakes." I nod earnestly. . . . Actually I'd forgotten about the cupcakes. "So I'm going to perform on my own at the concert and look like a total dork, but it's a sacrifice I'm willing to make to help you get it on with Toby." She flops next to me on the bed. Bill still has his back to us as he fiddles with leads. "I know how much you like Toby, and you were right. I'd probably dump a friend for a kiss."

"Slapsies?" Bill asks, turning round.

"Of course," I say. "When you play slapsies," I explain to Kat, "James Bond's weapon isn't a Kalashnikov—it's a great big hand that he goes round slapping baddies with instead."

"Like a James Bond bitch fight?"

"Exactly . . . but with explosions."

The three of us settle on the floor with Kat in the middle, and pretty soon we're having a surprisingly good Saturday night.

"So," says Kat, as she dies for the seventeenth time, "how did you and the T-Dog get along today?"

"It was fun," I say. Then, because she is clearly expecting more, I add, "He bought some sneakers."

"So romantic."

"And he gave me this." I show her my necklace.

"Really?" Now she's interested. She drops her controller to examine it. "He's basically saying you're his *fox*, Betty. OMG." Her eyes light up with excitement. "He bought you jewelry. That means you're his *girlfriend*!"

I gasp. Is she right? Then I gasp again. When I wasn't concentrating, Bill's character snuck up on mine and slapped me round the back of the head. "Bill, you've totally killed me!"

"Sorry," he says.

"You made my head explode!"

He gets up. "I think I'm going to head out."

"Don't go," says Kat. "We promise not to talk about

girlie stuff." But Bill's made up his mind because he's already pulling on his hoodie.

"Do you want me to walk you home?" he asks Kat.

"Okay," she says. Then she turns and faces me and mouths, "*Oh my God*," her eyes wide with excitement.

It looks like it's just going to be me and Dennis for the rest of the evening. Before they leave, I ask Bill for another quote. "Bill's educating me about love," I explain to Kat. I turn to a fresh page in my book and find my best inky pen. "He's cleverer than he looks," I add.

He pauses in the doorway for a moment and looks at me. "This is from a poem by Yeats—"

"Spell it," I interrupt.

"*Y. E. A. T. S.*"

"Got it," I say. "Go on."

"So he's talking to this woman who had a lot of admirers—"

"A hottie?" asks Kat.

"I guess she was probably a hottie."

"Like Beyoncé?"

"Probably a bit less hot than Beyoncé. Anyway, he says to her that when she is old, and thinking back over her life, there is one thing she must remember. . . ."

"What?" asks Kat, getting into the game.

"That although many men loved her beauty"—he pauses, looks at me, and I get ready to write—"*but one man loved the pilgrim soul in you.*"

I scribble this down. "I don't get it," says Kat.

"I do," I say. "I'm getting better at these. He's saying he saw beyond her hotness and truly loved her soul."

"But what's a pilgrim soul?" asks Kat.

Bill says, "A pilgrim is someone who follows their heart, like"—he looks round for inspiration then spots my Dora the Explorer ball hopper—"an explorer."

"So she's a cross between Beyoncé and Dora the Explorer," says Kat.

"You've got it," says Bill, smiling. They go downstairs, and soon I hear them calling good-bye to Dad and Rue.

When they've gone, my room seems very quiet, and I feel a bit lonely, particularly when I imagine Bill and Kat walking home together. I start to flick through my records. Mainly they're Dad's, but Gramps has also given me some. I know what I'm looking for. I pull out a bright yellow album. I always liked it when I was little because it's the color of Mr. Happy. On the front is a photograph of a black woman with bobbed hair, wearing a shirt with the pointiest collar I've ever seen. She's lying in a field of daffodils. Bettye Swann—my namesake and Mum's hero.

I clean the record with a drop of oil on a special cloth, making sure I do it just the way Dad taught me. This record is very old. Gently, I release the needle and, after a crackle of static, her rich voice fills my room.

I haven't listened to these songs for years. I take off my necklace and copy the curled-up fox into Dennis. I do a speech bubble coming out of its mouth so the fox is saying Bill's pilgrim quote. Does this necklace mean I'm Toby's girlfriend? Maybe. I think about the Crazy Mouse and the feeling I get when I'm chugging straight up the track, heading toward the big drop, that exciting, scary feeling. If I think about Kat and Bill walking together through the dark streets, or Dad and Poo downstairs, the scary feeling inside me gets worse.

I turn Bettye up and think about Toby. How he looks at me with his pale blue eyes and how his mouth is always smiling, like he's thinking of something funny.

Job for Monday, I write in Dennis. *Find out if I'm Toby's girlfriend.*

11.

Next week, I study everything Toby says and does. We hang out together a lot, but Frank and Dexter are always with us, and if we're not rehearsing, we're playing *FIFA 14*. Toby always makes me play with Dexter because I suck at soccer games. By Thursday, when I'm sitting in the hall with Kat waiting for a meeting about the Autumn Celebration to start, I still don't know if I'm his girlfriend.

As Mr. Simms starts talking, Toby slips into the seat next to me. Then—and I watch this happen—his hand falls on my knee . . . *and he leaves it there.* Toby is *holding* my knee in public.

My cartilage tingles with pleasure, and I struggle to sit still as Mr. Simms starts running through rehearsal schedules. "Remember, the concert is a week away, next Thursday," says Mr. Simms.

Very interesting, sir, but, right now, Toby is melting my body from my left knee upward, and it is rather distracting. Surely only boyfriends or creepy men put their hands on girls' knees? He must be my boyfriend. I think I have a boyfriend!

I'm just about holding it together, but Kat is sitting on the other side of me, and she isn't holding it together at all. The moment Toby's hand landed on my knee, she started digging me in my ribs with her finger, and it's getting painful. I stare straight ahead, refusing to look at her. My knee is being held by Toby, and my ribs are being prodded by Kat.

Then Toby leans toward me and whispers, "You all right, wifey?"

"Oh . . . great," I say.

Kat can't cope with this. The exact moment Toby says *wifey*, she begins to quiver with silent laughter.

"Calm down, Kat Knightley," says Mr. Simms.

"Yes," I say. "Calm down, *Kat*."

A minute later, I feel my phone vibrate. Kat's sent me a text: **wifey omg that means GIRLFRIEND i heard it on eastenders :D**

Kat shakes for the rest of the meeting while I sit like a statue, trying to stop her vibrations from traveling through my body and into Toby's hand. I don't want Toby thinking he makes me shake.

As everyone starts to leave, she leans around me and says, "You okay, Toby?"

"More than okay," he says. "My mum and stepdad are going away this weekend, so you know what that means. . . ."

"Party?" asks Kat.

"Partaaay!" he corrects. "There is going to be one huge party at my place this Saturday." He looks at me. "You coming, B-Cakes?"

"Yeah," I say, "I love parties." My heart is hammering. A party . . . surely this will mean a kiss? I am so glad I practiced kissing on all those Granny Smiths.

"How about you, Kat?" he asks.

"Sorry, I'm busy."

"Well, you're missing out," he says, getting up. "It's gonna be hectic—an all-nighter. Don't forget we're rehearsing after school, Betty. It's just us. I told Frank and Dexter we're going to work on your vocals." Then he gets to his feet, slowly stretches—giving Kat a nice view of his flat stomach—and walks out of the hall. At the door, he glances back and smiles.

"I wish you could come," I say to Kat. "I'm going to need moral support. I have a powerful premonition that I will be kissed on Saturday." I try to smile when I say this, but the idea is actually a bit scary.

"It might be weird if I'm sitting next to you for your first kiss," says Kat. "C'mon. Let's go to the cafeteria. I'm hungry."

I follow her out of the hall. My knee is still a bit wobbly. "What are you doing on Saturday?"

She pauses at the door. "I'm going windsurfing with Bill."

"What?" I say, amazed. "*You* are going *windsurfing* with Bill? Kat, you hate getting wet—rain makes you scream—and you fear exercise. I'm fairly certain windsurfing involves a lot of getting wet and exercise."

"You don't mind, do you, Betty?" she says. "I know he's your best friend, but he told me he was running this beginners' course on Saturday, and I asked if I could go, kind of as a joke, and then he said yes . . . and I thought, why not?"

" 'Course I don't mind," I say. We push our way down the corridor toward the canteen. Honestly? Part of me does mind. I suppose I don't like the idea of sharing Bill, a bit like how I don't want to share Dad. But I'm trying hard at the moment not to be selfish, particularly with Kat. "You'll have fun," I say. "He's always trying to get me to learn. So do you actually want to windsurf, or do you just want to check out Bill in a wet suit?"

"Hmm," she says. "I'd have to say a little bit from column A, and a bigger bit from column B." She smiles to herself and then goes a pretty shade of pink. I've seen Kat talk about boys loads, but she's never been *shy* before.

"Why can't you come to Toby's party in the evening? You could bring Bill."

"There's a barbecue afterward, and I'm getting a lift home with Bill. We'll be back too late."

"Wow . . . windsurfing . . . barbecue . . . that all sounds kind of *dateish*," I say, getting out my phone.

"What're you doing?"

"I'm going to call Bill and destroy him."

"No, you're not!" says Kat, and she gets her phone out.

"What are *you* doing?"

"Putting a totally public message on your timeline: *Good luck for your massive kiss with Toby, Betty,*" she says as she taps away. "*Just think, in two days' time, you'll no longer be a kissing virg—*" But that's all she gets to write because at that moment I grab her phone and run down the corridor with it. By the time she's caught up with me, I've dropped it into some passing boy's bag.

For the rest of lunchtime, Kat makes me walk around the school ringing her number, until we hear a drunk Smurf trapped in a seventh grader's backpack.

"Sorry," says Kat, unzipping his bag and pulling out her phone. "A very silly girl put this in your bag."

Before I go into Toby's garage after school, I take a deep breath. Knowing it will just be the two of us makes me nervous. Usually when we're rehearsing we walk to his place together, straight from school. Today, he wasn't waiting in our usual spot, so I came over on my own. I see him lying on the sofa, strumming his guitar.

"Hey," he says, glancing up. "I think we should make this a quickie." He glances at his phone, then drops it back on the sofa. "You stand over there, and I'll play from here."

I leave my bag by the door but keep my coat on. It's cold in here. I go and stand in the middle of the room. I've sung "Shut Up!" so many times now, I could do it in my sleep. Toby plays the intro and then nods me in. Using the bored voice I know he likes, we run through the song, but I've sung only three lines when he stops me and makes me start again.

"Can you get into it a bit more?" he asks, leaning back on the sofa and frowning. "Like move around, or something."

"Like this?" I say, running my hands up and down my body and wriggling about. I start to laugh. "Or this?" I do a dance I've seen Bea's sister do. It's like a robot twerking.

Toby smiles. "No, not really like that."

I shrug. "How d'you mean?"

"Like you're really *into* it."

I hesitate for a second and start to blush. I don't know why, but I feel stupid standing up with Toby watching me. The thing is, I'm not into the song—I never have been—but I am into being here with him. I'm just going to have to fake it. I guess my mum had to do this tons when she did gigs.

"All right, but I don't want you to watch." Toby rolls his eyes. "You come up here with me."

With a sigh, he flops off the sofa and comes to stand next to me. "Better?" he asks.

"Much."

He starts to play and I face his garage door, imagining it's our school hall, packed full of students and parents, and oh, Mrs. P., of course, watching me with a frown from the front row. I hang my head down and start to sing, "Shut up, shut up," through a curtain of hair, then I grab an imaginary microphone with both hands and clutch it to me as I sing the rest of the song.

The song finishes, and there's a moment's silence. I turn to face Toby.

"Nice," he says, looking at me with a smile. "You nailed it, B-Cakes."

"Yeah?"

Suddenly the garage is very quiet, and I have that feeling again—that *something* might happen, that I'm strapped in the Crazy Mouse and the carriage is heading for the big drop. I look at Toby's arms hanging down by the guitar. Do I want him to reach out for me? To pull me closer? He steps over a trailing wire, moving closer to me. Panic rises in my chest.

"I've got to go," I say in a rush.

He shrugs. "Don't forget my party on Saturday."

"I won't," I say as I grab my bag and head toward the door.

"You should stay over." Toby lazily strums a chord.

"What?"

"On Saturday. Everyone's going to crash here for the night." He slaps his hand down on the strings, and the hum of the guitar stops dead. I must look worried because he adds, "Mum's going to be around. It's just a sleepover."

"Oh, right," I say, as if having a sleepover at a boy's house is a totally normal thing to do. "If your mum's going to be here, I guess Dad won't mind." He would *massively* mind, and there is no way he can ever know about it. I wave good-bye to Toby and slip out of the garage.

I half walk, half run home, thinking about the lies I'm going to have to tell if I'm going to stay at Toby's on Saturday. Somehow I know that the kiss I've been waiting for will happen at the party, but maybe not if I have to leave before everyone else. Suddenly, there's one of Mum's letters I have to read.

Luckily, Dad's not in. Up in my room, I put on Bettye Swann and pull out the Puma box.

I hold *The one where I have my first kiss*. If I open this letter, then I'll have only one left. I dash out of my room, calling, "Mr. Smokey . . . I need you!" I find him asleep on a pair of Dad's pants. He digs his claws into them as I pick him up, so I'm forced to bring Mr. Smokey *and* Dad's pants back into my room.

"Sit on my knee and don't wriggle," I tell him. "I need your help . . . and Mum's." I open the letter, rest my chin on Mr. Smokey's head, and start to read.

Dear Plumface,

Kissing. I'll be honest; I was a bit of a late starter. My mum always used to say I was a "slow developer," you know, to the hairdresser, to my teachers at parents' evening, to my friends' mums (loudly, at parents' evening). She was probably right. I was a slow developer in all the key "becoming a woman" areas: bras, periods, and kissing. When I was fifteen, I dragged Mum to Marks & Spencer and forced her to buy me a bra. As the sales assistant was measuring me, I saw Mum shaking her head in the mirror, and then she whispered to the assistant, "They're just buds."

When the sales assistant announced I was "almost *a 28AA," Mum did an* I told you so *face, but she perked up when I was given the bras.*

"Oh my God!" she shrieked as I pulled the first one out of the packet. "It's so dinky . . . just like your first-ever shoes. Maybe I could get them framed together!" Seeing my disgusted face, she added, "A nice box *frame, Lorna. Something tasteful . . . it can go in the hallway."*

On to periods. Does the tampon lady still come into schools? I hope so because I can't imagine Dad sitting you down and explaining how a tampon works. When I was eleven, all the girls in my year were called to a special assembly. A lady wearing jeans and a fluffy sweater stood in front of us and showed us pictures of ovaries on the overhead projector.

"You will probably start your periods sometime before your fifteenth birthday," she announced cheerfully.

I can't remember much about the rest of the talk, except she held up a teacup and said that a whole period would fill up only half a teacup—I think that was supposed to reassure us—and that when we first tried to use a tampon, we should take a pet into the toilet to help us relax. I don't think I've made the last bit up.

Anyway, me and Mrs. Miggins (my hamster) waited and waited for the big day. Finally, when I was about one week off my fifteenth birthday, I saw a tiny brown spot in my underwear. YES!!!! I rushed out of the toilet and got my hamster. Now Gramps had made quite a complicated living arrangement for Mrs. Miggins: two double-story cages joined by a tunnel. Laboriously, I moved her home into the toilet then squeezed in next to the cages.

Mrs. Miggins climbed to the top of one of her cages and hung by two paws, swinging and watching me with her beady black eyes. She was making me feel self-conscious, so I gave her some toilet paper to distract her. She started shredding it and stuffing it in her cheeks. I squeezed down onto the floor next to her and watched her for a while. Then I picked up my mum's Take a

Break *magazine. I was starting to feel relaxed . . . maybe that tampon lady knew what she was talking about.*

When we emerged from the toilet an hour later, I'd had zero tampon success, but Mrs. Miggins had made a huge nest, and I'd read about a woman who had a growth removed from her stomach. The growth was exactly *the same shape as Italy!*

On to the main event. Kissing. When I was sixteen and a half, my class had a Christmas party. I was certain that every girl in my year had been kissed by now, and I was getting desperate. I decided that, no matter what, I was going to kiss someone at the party. Unfortunately, there was no one going who I wanted to kiss. This didn't put me off. My best friend, Julia, decided I was more likely to be kissed if my legs were perfectly smooth. She got a tube of her mum's depilatory cream and told me it would dissolve all my unwanted hair. We sat on the edge of the bath and smothered our legs in it. This stuff was slippery, and we were using a lot of it, and at one point I slipped into the bath. Julia told me to stop messing around, and in the general confusion (we were listening to Guns N' Roses and putting on mud face masks), neither of us noticed the blob of cream on my head.

I lost a small patch of hair—about the size of a coin—and Julia quickly rearranged my hair into a very unfashionable side bunch. I looked in the mirror. The overall effect wasn't great—a white patch of scalp still gleamed through my hair, but Julia swore no one would notice in the darkness of the club. I didn't want to go, but Julia said she'd kill me if I abandoned her, so we set off across town, dressed up in our coolest clothes (DMs, black tights, flowery dresses) and drenched in Body Shop Dewberry perfume.

As we lined up to get into the club, I started chatting to a boy from my History class—I didn't fancy him or anything, but I was thinking, You'll do. *He was telling me about his Saturday job when he suddenly stopped talking and gazed intently at my head.*

"What's that?" he asked, pointing at my hair.

"What?" I felt the smooth bald patch with my fingers and quickly pulled my hair back over it. "Oh, that's just my . . . scalp spot. All the girls are doing it. It's like being blood brothers, but instead we're scalp sisters." He frowned and glanced around at the other girls standing near us in the line. "Most of them have got one," I said.

When we got in the club, I told Julia that she was getting a scalp spot tomorrow or I was going straight home. She agreed, but to be honest she'd have agreed to anything by then because she'd drunk two bottles of Boone's Farm and was very overexcited. Giggling, she dragged me over to a booth, and soon I found myself sitting next to history boy. We smiled and shouted at each other for a few minutes, and then he moved toward me, getting closer and closer, until I went cross-eyed trying to focus on him. The next thing I knew, our lips were touching and, amazingly, I was being kissed! I sat there with my mouth slightly open, and it was just about bearable until he started pushing his tongue in and out of my mouth. His tongue tasted of pretzels.

"Sorry," I said, gasping for fresh, pretzel-free air, "but I feel sick." Then I hid in the bathroom until Gramps arrived to take me home.

If I'd thought things through, I wouldn't have had a disastrous first kiss with a boy who I had to sit next to in History on Monday morning . . . and for the next two years.

Now I'm going to tell you a BIG secret. A few months later, it was Carlo's birthday. Being an all-around wonderful person, he was having a bonfire on the beach to celebrate. It was a cold night, and a few people had ducked out, including Eleanor, so by the end of the evening, there were only a handful of us sitting round the glowing embers.

Carlo and I went down to the water's edge to have a pebble-skimming competition. The moon was low and full, and it shone a silver path across the sea. A thousand stars were scattered across the sky. What I'm saying, Betty, is that it was romantic. *Carlo and I looked at each other. He put his hands on either side of my face, and I slipped mine round his waist. Our whole bodies were touching, and I could feel his heart beating fast. He kissed me, and I kissed him, and I never wanted it to end. The sea rolled and crashed, again and again, and I melted into our kiss, and although I was drifting off on a cloud of happiness, I managed to notice that Carlo's mouth tasted of Werther's Originals. That was my first* real *kiss. History boy didn't count, because I didn't kiss him back.*

I'm not sure what my message is here, Plumface. Perhaps I should summarize the key points for you:

- *Don't take Nanna bra shopping.*
- *Never try to use a tampon if a live animal is in the same room.*
- *Kissing someone you like is as natural as laughing. Kissing someone you don't like is as unnatural as putting your tongue into a stranger's mouth. (And letting them stick their tongue into yours.)*

Actually, toddler-you is sucking my chin right now, so I'm going to have to stop writing. If your kissing technique doesn't improve in the next few years, when you do kiss someone for the first time, aim a little higher. And don't *suck.*

Love you always,
Mumface xx

That's the longest letter Mum's written me. I press the sheets of paper out flat and put them into Dennis. If Mum had never died, if she was downstairs in the kitchen making me dinner, would she tell me these things?

I've got no photos of Mum in my room, so I go into the hallway and take my favorite one off the wall. She's standing under a blue sky, and the wind is blowing back her blond hair. She's wearing a stripy polo shirt, unbuttoned, and looking off to one side, smiling her big smile. I used to imagine she was looking at me, but she looks too young. I put the photo on my bedside table, next to my fox necklace, and that's all it takes to make my mind fly back to Toby and his curving smile and wild black hair.

After turning Mum's photo slightly away so I'm not being watched, I lie facedown on my pillow and practice kissing. I try really hard not to suck. After a while, I realize I can't breathe, so I come up for air.

No way am I eating pretzels at Toby's party.

12.

When I come down to breakfast on Saturday morning, I find Poo sitting in front of a big stack of pancakes. She's been around here a lot this week, and now she's wriggled her way into breakfast as well. I sit at the other end of the table and get out my phone.

"Put it away," says Dad.

"Hang on," I say, "just got a message."

A shiver of excitement runs through me when I see Toby's name. I open the message: **Looking forward to tonight . . . x** He's attached a photo, but as usual my antique phone is letting me down and I can't see it yet. It'll probably appear in a week.

"Betty!"

"One minute." **Me too x B**, I reply. I drop my phone on the table and glance down at Poo's feet. Good. She's wearing shoes, so she's only just arrived. So far, they haven't subjected me to Poo staying the night, but I can sense they are building up to it. Actually, their gross middle-aged lust might help me out. . . .

"Dad," I say, as he passes me my pancakes, "can I stay at Kat's tonight?"

"Okay," he says, then I'm sure I catch him flicking Poo a look. I force myself to smile at her. She's already looking at me, with her calm, knowing look.

"Nice pancakes?" I ask sweetly.

"Lovely," she says, taking a bite and smiling, all at the same time.

"So I've got a pair of pajamas, a toothbrush, hairbrush, deodorant," I say to Bea, pointing at each item in turn, "and Cheerios." I give the Tupperware box a shake, and the cereal rattles around.

"Why do you have Cheerios?" she asks. She's rolling a seamed stocking up her leg, busy transforming herself into a 1950s starlet for Hollywood Night at her jive club.

"For breakfast," I say. "In case Toby only has stuff like raisin bran." I start to pack all my things back into my duck backpack.

"So you're really staying the night?"

"Yep, it'll be fine. His mum's going to be there." Bea

pulls on a purple dress and starts to do her makeup. I squeeze next to her so I can share her stuff. I'm around here because it's on the way to Toby's, and Dad would have got suspicious if I was all dressed up to stay the night at Kat's. I decided it was too risky to tell him I was sleeping at Bea's because she's incapable of lying.

"It's just," she says, looking at me in the mirror, "you could always change your mind."

"I'm not going to change my mind. It'll be fun," I say. I stand up and give her a twirl. "Do you like my kissing outfit?" I'm wearing yellow DMs and a knitted dress with skulls all over it. It's not as scary as it sounds, because the skulls are smiling.

"I'd kiss you."

"Thanks!" I look at the time. I can't go yet—it's too early. "I wish I had someone to walk in with," I say.

"As soon as you see Toby, you'll be fine," she says. She starts to make her lips bright red. "So tonight could be *the night.*"

"The night I am kissed," I say, my voice a bit flat.

"Excited?"

"Yes . . . definitely excited." I lean over her shoulder. Our faces are close together in the mirror. "Can you do that on me?" Bea gets out a tiny pencil and draws an outline round my lips. Then she fills it in with a brush. I watch in the mirror as a sweeping red smile appears on my face. I'm wearing my hair down, and my only other makeup is eyeliner and mascara. My long, straight bangs hide the tops of my eyes.

Bea sits back and studies me. "It looks nice," she says. "It goes with your freckles."

Suddenly, a warm little hand pats my leg, and I look down to see Emma lying on the floor, staring up at me with a crazy look in her eyes. She's wearing a curly blond wig.

"Emma's into creeping up on people at the moment," explains Bea. "The other night she got into the shower with me, and I only noticed when I stepped on her."

"Hello, Betty," says Emma, stroking my leg. "Your tights are soft."

"Thanks," I say. I pull on my panda hat. I've decided I'm going to walk to Toby's very slowly.

"Will you suck my finger?" Emma asks, sticking her finger up at me.

"Whatever you do, don't suck her finger," says Bea.

"I think I'll pass tonight, Emma."

"Why?" She looks at the end of her finger, trying to work out what's wrong with it.

"Because I've got a very important date with a first kiss," I say. Then I smile a brave red smile and wave good-bye.

I take my time getting to Toby's, making a little detour to the park, where I go on the swings for a while. I swing really high to get my adrenaline levels up and to keep my smile in place, but by the time I'm walking down Toby's street, the smile has disappeared, and I've developed total kissing-fright. I pass dark houses, sweeping drives, and high metal gates. My footsteps echo on the pavement, and my stomach churns with anxiety. To distract myself, I think about Kat and Bill, wondering how her windsurfing lesson went and if they're having their barbecue by the beach. I imagine the coals glowing, their cold fingers wrapped round sizzling food.

Too soon, I'm standing outside Toby's front door. It's huge, like the door to a giant's castle. I can hear the distant *thud, thud, thud* of dance music. I pull off my hat and sort out my hair. Then I take a deep breath and ring the bell.

There's no answer. I try the door and it swings open.

Even though we've had rehearsals in the garage, this is the first time I've ever been inside Toby's house. In front of me is a shining wooden floor and a wide flight of stairs covered in a deep red carpet. Cinderella could sweep down these stairs. There's even a chandelier hanging above me, filling the hallway with a warm glow.

I dump my stuff by a pile of coats and head toward the noise. I walk into a lounge heaving with teenagers. A few I recognize from school—Jess Cobb is laughing hysterically at something a boy in a rugby shirt is saying—but most of them I've never seen before. I guess Toby's mainly invited friends from his old school. I spot him in the corner of the room, fiddling with his iPod. His hair is carefully styled, and he's wearing a shirt with half the buttons undone.

Bea's right. I do feel fine now that I've seen him. Better than fine. Quickly I work my way through a group of dancing girls.

"Hey!" I say, standing in front of him. He looks at me and grins.

For a moment I feel shy, but then he clutches me to him and says, "B-Cakes!" into my hair. Keeping me squeezed against his chest, he starts dancing with me and singing along to the music. I laugh, and just as I'm wondering why he's being so affectionate, I see the beer bottle in his hand.

"Where's your mum?" I ask.

"Decided to go out," he says. "But she took me shopping first, so we've got everything we need." He waves his bottle around.

"Toby!" yells a voice from the door, and he lets go of me. "Get a drink," he calls over his shoulder as he goes to see his friend.

Everyone in the kitchen seems to know one another. I try to be smiley, but they're heavily into a conversation about someone named Sophie the Slagasaurus and a stolen lip gloss, and they all ignore me. I search through the half-empty plastic bags that are stacked along the countertop and grab a bottle of watermelon Bacardi Breezer.

By the time I get back to the lounge, Toby is dancing in the middle of the room with a group of girls. Just by looking at them, I can tell they're different from me. Everything about them shimmers—their hair, their lips, their clothes. I take a sip of my warm drink and force myself to smile. Why should I worry? I'm Toby's B-Cakes, the singer in his band, the girl he buys jewelry for.

I give the pointy nose of my fox necklace a stroke and drop down on a huge white sofa. The Bacardi Breezer tastes like cough syrup and is making me feel sick. I shouldn't have skipped dinner tonight. I've only drunk a couple of times before—at a party Ollie had and Gramps's seventieth. When Dad caught me drinking sparkling wine at Gramps's, he said I was poisoning my body, so I don't think he'd be too happy about this.

"Hello," says a voice from my side. I turn round. I do know someone else at this party. Pearl is sitting next to me on the sofa, half-buried under scattered cushions and discarded cardigans.

"Hey," I say cautiously. I'm so desperate to talk to someone that I'm almost pleased to see her . . . not something I've felt for a long time. She's got a heart-shaped cushion clutched to her stomach, and her feet are up on a coffee table. She looks at me through her thick black eye makeup, a bored expression on her face. Her skin and lips are as pale as the sofa we're sitting on.

"You all right?" she says.

"I'm okay," I say, then we both go back to watching the dancers. "How come you're here?" I ask after a minute. "I didn't think Toby was your favorite person."

"I think he's a dumbass," she says, "but I don't like hanging around at home."

"So where are Lauren and Holly?" The three of them are usually joined at the hip, but, come to think of it, Pearl's been on her own a bit recently.

"They're mad with me. I signed Mrs. P. up to a cougar dating site—"

"A what?"

"Cougar—a dating site for men who like mature ladies, like Mrs. P."

"That's funny," I say.

"Well, they didn't think so," she says, rolling her eyes. "I used Lauren's school account . . . and Holly's name."

"Still funny."

"They got expelled from school for a week."

"Oh."

"And there was some other stuff . . . on Facebook. Stuff I wrote about them." Pearl has a small pile of peanuts on the cushion. She starts flicking them across the room. One pings off a girl's skinny-jeaned bottom, and Pearl sniggers. "Urrh," she says. "Look at that loser."

"Who?" I say, following her eyes. "Toby?"

She grins and looks at me sideways. "Now, why would I be talking about Toby? You fancy him *so* much!" Then she points into the crowd with a bottle of vodka. “No. That’s the loser . . . my brother.”

I see Pearl’s older brother, Alfie, at the edge of the room. He’s got a cigarette hanging out of his mouth, and he’s dancing on his own. It’s hard to see what’s annoyed her so much, but when he sees her watching him, his eyes narrow and he stares at her cruelly. Then, still staring at Pearl, he stubs out his cigarette on the side of the mantelpiece, leaving a black circle.

I haven’t had anything to do with Alfie for years. When we were little, he was always freaking out at us for touching his dinosaurs. He loved dinosaurs. Then I think of something Pearl and I did to Alfie. Something so funny, I have to share it with her. “Pearl, do you remember when we stapled Alfie’s clothes all over your house?”

She thinks for a moment, then snorts and clutches her hand to her mouth to stop herself from spraying drink all over the sofa. “You stapled his pants to the stairs!”

“And his socks to his bedroom door, and we filled them with his dinosaurs,” I say. “We’d never used a stapler before. It was fun.”

“How old were we?”

“Five,” I say.

“After your dad picked you up, Alfie stapled my finger.” She points at a tiny white mark just under her nail.

“What?”

"Not really," she says. Then she laughs and lets her head flop back on the sofa.

Pearl and I hang out for ages, chatting about when we were little and playing some skillful games like Get the Peanut in the Coke Bottle, and Would You Rather. . . .

"Okay," says Pearl, "this one is hard. Would you rather *dance* naked or *bowl* naked?"

"Tricky," I say. "Any type of dance?"

"Energetic disco dance."

"Bowl. I reckon I could do it gracefully, but I definitely wouldn't use the between-your-legs technique."

Pearl laughs and feels about under the sofa. Eventually she pulls out two more bottles, but this time it's beer. "You want one?"

I nod, and she opens them with a Homer Simpson bottle opener she's got tucked under her cushion. The beer tastes even worse than the Bacardi Breezer, but at least it's distracting me from the sight of Toby, who's now paired up with a girl in a strappy black-and-silver playsuit.

"So you going out with Toby or what?" asks Pearl as the girl loops her arms round Toby's neck.

"Kind of," I say, but then I see Toby's hands fall onto the girl's hips, and I watch as he draws her closer to him. An icy sickness creeps through me. All I can do is sip my disgusting beer and keep telling myself that they're probably old mates, just like me and Bill. Only I'd never do that with Bill.

I get out my phone to see if he's texted me. I'm curious to know how he's getting on with Kat. Nothing, but Toby's picture has finally come through. I open his message, and the picture appears, pixel by pixel. My phone is so annoying.

At first, all I see is his dark hair, and then his blue eyes are staring straight at me. Next, his grin and then . . .

"Oh my God!" gasps Pearl, peering over my shoulder. Together we watch as Toby's naked torso fills the screen. I slam my phone facedown on my lap and feel my cheeks burn. "Are you two *sexting* each other?"

"What?" I say. "I mean, no!" Even though I'm not looking at the screen, I can still see his pale chest, his nipples, and, peeking out of the top of his jeans, the elastic on his *boxers*. "We've never even kissed," I say, knowing how pathetic I sound.

"Well, he's sexting *you*."

The room seems to spin. This photo changes the meaning of **Looking forward to tonight x**.

"He should be going out with someone like me," says Pearl flatly. And, just as I'm thinking, *What am I doing here, talking to this girl who hates me and wants to steal my boyfriend?* she adds, "You shouldn't be chasing a dumbass like that." Then she pulls herself forward and gets unsteadily to her feet. "Laters, Sweaty," she says, then ruffles my hair and wanders off in the direction of the kitchen.

Someone has turned the music up. I feel dizzy, so I lean

back and stare at the ceiling. I think about what Pearl said. Why would she want to go out with someone she doesn't even like? Turning my phone over, I try to look at the photo like I'm looking at my boyfriend, but I just feel embarrassed, so I turn my phone off.

"Dude!" The chest, thankfully clothed, looms over me. "Been looking for you, B-Cakes."

"Been right here," I say. "Just watching the dancing."

He grabs me by the hand and pulls me to my feet. "Come on," he says. "Let's get out of here." Then he leads me through the dancers, across the polished hall, and up the Cinderella stairs. As the high ceiling flies past, my heart speeds up. It's going to happen. I know it is. The thing I've wanted to happen since the moment I set eyes on him . . . so why do I want to run back downstairs to Pearl?

"Where are we going?"

"Tour of the house," says Toby.

Because his house has about seven bedrooms, the tour takes quite a long time. Eventually, he leads me down a dimly lit corridor and up a second, narrower flight of stairs. It's quiet up here and much cooler.

"Shouldn't we get back to the others?" I hold on tight to his hand because we seem to be moving too fast, and my legs are wobbly.

"They won't even notice we're gone." We stop outside a door. "Behold, B-Cakes," he says, pushing open the door. "The Toby cave!"

I walk in, and he shuts the door behind me. The sounds of the party disappear. His room doesn't seem to fit with the perfection of the rest of the house. The walls are dark red, and I have to pick my way over dropped T-shirts and jeans. I start to look around. Toby follows close behind. I hesitate by his desk and see a pile of abandoned books and some dirty plates.

"I'm reading this in English," I say, picking up *Of Mice and Men*, but Toby ignores me and steps a little closer. I move away. "I like the bit about the dog . . . I mean, it's sad, but it's good."

Toby's got only two posters on the wall. One's from the second Hunger Games film. It's falling down in one corner, so I stick it back up. The other one, the one over his bed, has VARIOUS BABES written across the bottom. Toby sits down on his bed, and I look closer. It's a photo of five women standing in a row, all thrusting their hips out at sharp angles. They're wearing undone denim hot pants and vest tops, and they're staring and snarling through manes of glossy hair.

They look like the type of girl every boy is supposed to fancy. They look *nothing* like me.

"Sit down," says Toby, patting his Union Jack duvet cover. My heart starts to thud, and I drift over to his bookcase. On the top shelf is a row of model cars, all carefully arranged and pointing in the same direction. "This is cool," I say, picking up a little VW camper van.

"Its doors open," he says. I use the tip of my nail to flip the back door open and shut.

Then, because I can't put it off any longer, I go and sit next to him. Close, but not too close.

"So"—I stare down at my feet—"when's your mum coming back?"

"Not for ages." He shifts closer to me. I don't dare look at him, because I can tell he's staring at me, and I know I'm going red.

I search the room, desperate to find something else to talk about. Spotting the Hunger Games poster again, I turn to him and say, "Did you—" But Toby is suddenly in front of my face.

"Shh," he says, leaning against me. I lose my balance and fall back on the bed. I go to laugh, but Toby presses against me more and his breath is on my face and his lips are touching mine. I try to shift sideways because my arm is trapped under me, and then his tongue pushes into my mouth. Our teeth bang together, and I feel Toby's heart beating fast.

Suddenly I want to cry, and as I'm pressed further into the duvet, I see Katniss over Toby's shoulder shooting a flaming arrow right at me. Katniss is kicking ass. I'm just lying here having my face kissed. I don't like this!

"Toby . . ." I try to pull my arm out.

"What?" he says breathlessly, barely listening, his lips all over the side of my face.

"Stop it!" I say. I wriggle out from under him and off the bed.

"What's wrong?"

"Nothing." I try to smile. "It's just that my arm hurt and—"

"God, Betty," he says, getting up. He glances in a mirror and sorts out his hair. "You," he says, laughing, "are just so weird." Then he pushes past me and walks toward the door, kicking a guitar out of his way. "Don't hang around up here," he says. Then he's gone.

Shame rushes through me. I pull my dress down and wipe my mouth where I can tell my red lipstick is smudged. I wait a few seconds, my heart pounding, and then I creep along the corridor, down the narrow steps, and then down the curved staircase. My hand shakes on the banister. Quickly, I grab my coat and bag from the pile in the hallway and let myself out of the house.

As I walk down the driveway, I start to cry, and then, when I get to the road, I start to run. I can't go home. I never want Dad to know about this party or what just happened. Rain hits my face and I keep running, turning left, then right, not thinking about where I'm going or stopping when I get a stitch. I don't care where I end up—I just want to get as far away from Toby's house as possible.

13.

It's only when I stop running that I realize I'm lost. I wander around, trying not to panic, desperately trying to spot a street or building I recognize. Eventually, I realize I'm on the edge of town, somewhere I've never been before. I peer over a hedge into a sports field. The houses stopped a while back, and I'm not even on a proper road anymore. It's quiet out here. And dark. Beyond the field, black trees bend in the wind. The drizzle hasn't stopped, so I walk toward a cricket pavilion in the corner of the field. I can see a bench lit up by a blue security light.

I perch on the edge of the wet bench and try to open my bag. I need to look at my phone and work out where I am. It's hard to do anything because my hands are so cold. Right at the top of my bag are my tub of Cheerios and

Pingu pajamas. They make me feel stupid all over again. I push them aside and feel for my phone.

Suddenly, I freeze. I can hear something: the purr of an engine.

I hold my breath and listen as it gets louder.

Then I see a van driving alongside the field, its headlights beaming over the top of the hedge. I pray for it to pass, but it gets slower and slower and then comes to an abrupt stop. The engine cuts out, and for a moment everything is silent.

I hardly dare to breathe. Is someone in the van watching me?

Suddenly I feel very alone, sitting on this bench in the middle of nowhere. I find my phone, pull it out, and turn it on. *Come on, come on.* I glance back and forth from the screen to the van. Then, just as the screen finally lights up, I hear the van door click open. I grab my bag, jump off the bench, and run round the side of the pavilion.

Spotting two trash cans, I squeeze in between them. I crouch down and lean forward, staring at the entrance to the field, my heart beating hard.

Silently, a dark figure steps through the gate. It's a man, and he's tall and wearing a big coat. He stands there, hands on hips, looking slowly from left to right, scanning the field. What's he doing? He turns toward the pavilion, and I shrink back. Did he follow me here? I feel sick with fear and clumsily tap my password into my phone, but my fingers won't work properly, and I keep getting it wrong.

Heavy panting comes out of nowhere, and I drop my phone with a clatter. A fat white dog sticks its face between the bins and stares at me, tongue hanging out, saliva dripping on my boots, a growl coming from deep in its throat. Slowly, I pick up my phone. Then I make my hand into a fist and stretch it toward the dog.

"Nice doggy," I whisper, my voice shaking. It sniffs my hand, then disappears as quickly as it appeared.

I sink back into the gap, but suddenly the drooling dog is back, and this time it barks so loud I feel the vibrations in my chest.

"Get here!" shouts the man, and I hear him stomp closer.

I have to call someone! I scroll through my address book, my thumb clumsy on the screen. The second I see Bill's name, I hit call. *C'mon, Bill. Please have your phone on.* It rings once, twice, three times. I peer out. The man is standing in the middle of the field, staring in my direction. *Pick up, Bill!* I watch him light a cigarette—the glowing tip waves in the darkness.

"Betty?" Bill's voice is muffled, like he's far away.

"Bill," I whisper, relief flooding my body. As soon as I've said this, I put my hand over my mouth, trying to keep a scared sob inside me.

"What's the matter?" He's clearer now, more awake. "I can't hear you."

"I'm in a field between two trash cans," I say, "and there's a big man here and his dog and they won't go away!"

"Tell me where you are," says Bill. As quietly as I can, I describe the cricket pavilion, the woods, and the dead-end road. "I know where you are," he says.

"Thank you," I whisper, but the line's gone dead. I make myself as small as possible and hug my knees. My heart is still pounding, and I pray the shadow of the man doesn't fall across the slice of sky between the two bins.

A few minutes later, a low whistle cuts through the night air, followed by a scamper of legs. Then I hear the van door slam shut and the engine start. I listen as it reverses down the track, turns, then accelerates away. I uncurl and peep out of the gap. That's when I see Bill bombing across the field, standing up as he peddles, beanie pulled low over his ears. I'm so relieved, I start crying all over again.

I crawl out of the space as he comes to a stop in front of me. "Hello," he says, peering down. He rests on his handlebars, trying to catch his breath. I stand up and his eyes widen. "What happened to you?"

"I got lost." I wipe away my smudged makeup and peel a chip bag off my leg. We stand looking at each other for a moment. More than anything I want to throw my arms round him, but this isn't the sort of thing we do. Instead I say, "I'm so happy to see you," and try to smile.

He frowns. Bill frowns a lot, but this is a particularly long one. "Why aren't you at the party?"

"I didn't like it," I say, tugging the pom-poms that hang from my hat, "so I left, but then I got lost." Bill's still on his bike, waiting for me to explain, like we've got all the time in the world and it's not one in the morning. "Can I stay at your place?" I ask. "Dad thinks I'm at Kat's. If I go home, he'll kill me."

He studies me for a moment longer. "Okay," he says. "Climb on."

I sit on the seat and put my arms round his waist. After a brief wobble, we set off across the field. As soon as we leave the wet grass and hit the road, we speed up. Houses and streetlights flash past us, and the air feels so good on my face. "You should be wearing a helmet," I say.

"I left in a rush," he replies. I rest my head on his warm back and shut my eyes. I feel every bump in the road. "Where shall we go?" Bill asks. I lift up my head, and the street lamps make me feel dizzy. We've been playing this game since we were little. We'd be cycling through the woods, my dad trying to keep up with us, and we'd really believe we could just pedal up and away and go anywhere we wanted.

"The North Pole," I say to Bill's back. Toby's pale chest definitely won't be in the North Pole.

"We'll make an igloo," says Bill, puffing as we start to climb a hill.

"And fill it with furs and light a fire right in the middle of it . . ."

". . . and toast marshmallows," says Bill.

"Then," I say, "a talking snow monkey will knock on the door."

"Do igloos have doors?"

"Do snow monkeys talk?

Bill is puffing now, but he never quits on a hill. "And," he says, "he'd have a bag with him."

"What's in the bag?"

"A Wii . . . and a generator." With a final push, we crest the hill. "Hold on," he warns.

"What does the monkey say?" We zoom down the other side, my hair flying back from my face.

"Three-player Mario Kart, Betty? Mushroom Gorge?"

"Dibs, I'm Toad!"

At Bill's, I go straight to the bathroom, scrub my face, and change into my pajamas. As I pass Eric's room, I see him flopped on top of his quilt, fast asleep, his arms dangling over the side of his bed. A dim orange glow comes from his night-light.

I go into Bill's room and find him pulling a sleeping bag out of a cupboard. "Nice jim jams," he says.

I look down at the tiny Pingu parading across my pajamas. Suddenly I don't know what to do with myself, even though I'm usually totally relaxed round at Bill's. "I haven't stayed over at your house for years," I say. "Do you remember when your mum let us sleep in the bath?"

"Why did we want to do that?"

"I don't know."

"You can have the bed," he says. "I'll sleep on the sofa."

I climb into his bed and pull the duvet around my face. It is the nicest feeling.

"Don't go yet," I say.

He drops down next to me. "I think this is going to be a hard one to explain to Mum," he says. "You know, how you've suddenly appeared in my bed during the night."

"I'll think of something."

"I've got something to show you," says Bill. Then he reaches up to his hat.

"You haven't!"

"Yes, I have," he says, pulling off his hat. All his crazy blond hair has gone. Now it's short. Very short. He runs his hands through it, messing it up. "What d'you think?"

"I think," I say, reaching out and stroking his head, "nice." And it is. I tuck my hand back in the duvet, but I can't stop looking at him.

"What?"

"Nothing. You look different."

He leans on the bed and yawns. He looks exhausted. I guess he's been windsurfing all day and then someone woke him up.

"What happened at the party?" he asks. "I thought you were all having a sleepover." I groan and wriggle down under the duvet, hiding my face. "What're you doing?"

"I can't look at you if I'm going to talk about the party," I say. "It's too embarrassing."

"It can't have been that bad," he says. Because I'm hidden, I let a tear slip down my cheek. It wasn't that bad, was it? Just a horrible kiss when I thought it would be an amazing kiss. Just the feeling that there's something wrong with me because I didn't like it. "Are you still awake in there?"

"It wasn't what I expected," I say. Now I'm under the duvet, I don't want to come out. "Will you talk to me until I fall asleep?"

"What about?"

"Tell me about Kat learning to windsurf."

Somehow I know he's smiling. "There was a lot of screaming, and she had to be rescued by the speedboat a few times. But she was good for a beginner." And then he tells me all about how she got out on the sea and about the barbecue and someone named Mikey who played the didgeridoo. It's nice listening to him. "Syd got out her guitar, and then Kat sang some song about a pencil."

"Who's Syd?" I've never heard Bill mention a Syd before.

"Just a girl from windsurfing."

"Is she nice?"

"She's okay," says Bill. "But she's a close talker."

"How close?"

"Tonight I could see Pringles between her teeth."

"That's close," I say, feeling better. Then I shut my eyes for a few seconds, and I realize I'm falling asleep. "Give me another quote, Bill."

"What about?"

"Love. Tell me something that'll make me happy." I stick my arm out of the bed. "Write it on here," I say sleepily. "I'll copy it into Dennis in the morning."

I hear Bill looking for a pen, and then there's a pause. He holds my arm steady and starts writing at my elbow. It feels tickly.

"Sorry," he says. "It's pretty long."

"Have you finished your essay?" I ask. I close my eyes. Bill laughs and says something, but his voice slips away from me as I drift off to sleep.

The next morning, I wake up early, and for a few seconds I can't work out where I am. Then I see a windsurfing harness hanging off the back of a chair, and I know I'm at Bill's. Thoughts of last night flood through me. I see Toby's hands on the hips of that girl, the way her outfit sparkled, and then Toby squashing me on his bed.

My chest aches. Something feels bruised inside. I

remember Mum's last letter, *The one where I got my heart broken.* Is my heart broken?

I want to go home.

I get dressed in the dark and go downstairs. The living room door is shut, so Bill's probably still asleep. I slip out the front door. It's just starting to get light. As I walk down Bill's street, a bird starts singing its heart out like it's the best day in the world.

In a few minutes, I'm home and creeping past Dad's door. I go straight to the bathroom. Right now, I don't even care if Rue stayed the night. Turning on the shower, I pull my dress over my head, and then I see Bill's writing on my arm.

I tear a sheet out of Dad's sudoku book and copy the quote down. I think I've got it right. *I have spread my dreams under your feet; Tread softly because you tread on my dreams.* I need to ask Bill who wrote it. I think I know what it means.

I climb under the shower and make the water as hot as I can bear it. I squeeze loads of Dove shower gel onto a sponge and scrub myself until mounds of bubbles appear, but the ache inside me just won't go away.

Last night, when I went to the party, I had a dream and then somehow, because I did something wrong and was *weird*, my dream got trampled on. I make the water even hotter.

What's wrong with me? I've liked Toby since the

moment I set eyes on him, so why didn't I like kissing him? The water becomes a tiny bit cooler. I remember what Mum said in her letter, that kissing someone you don't like is *unnatural*. But I do like Toby, don't I? I like the way his hair flops down in front of his eyes and how I feel when I sit next to him. I like the way he plays the guitar. I even like the way he smells. Of course I like him. He's right. I'm just weird. Suddenly, all the warmth in the water disappears, and icy water pours over me. I rush to turn the shower off.

I wrap myself in a towel and sit on the edge of the bath, staring at the steamed-up mirror. Somehow, I've got to get Toby to give me another chance, so I can be his one and only B-Cakes again.

Then the ache will go away.

14.

"You've got to tell us all about it!" says Kat as we go into assembly. Kat and Bea take a seat on each side of me. "Did you kiss him?"

That is a really good question. Did I kiss Toby? Mum said history boy didn't count, because she didn't kiss him back.

"Are you okay, Betty?" asks Bea.

"Yeah, I'm fine," I say.

I'm not fine. I had to force myself to come to school this morning. The thought of seeing Toby makes me feel sick. I made such an idiot of myself. I don't know what I'll say when I see him, but somehow I can make things right. After all, we're performing in the concert together on Thursday. "I'm just tired," I say. "I slept most of yesterday."

"I sent you fifteen texts," says Bea.

"I know," I say. "I replied to them all."

"With fifteen photos of Mr. Smokey . . ."

"He's a cute cat."

"I wanted to know if you were okay."

"I'm okay." Students gradually fill up the seats behind us. A few vague details about Bacardi Breezers and chandeliers distract Kat and Bea from the big-kiss issue. I keep glancing back, looking for Toby, but I can't see him anywhere.

"Betty," says Kat, nudging me. "Is that Dexter's drum kit on the stage?"

I nod. "Weird," I say. Dexter has stenciled a lime-green *X* on each drum skin, and I'd recognize his kit anywhere. I look behind me again for Toby and see Pearl slip into the hall by a side door. She slumps down in the last seat in our row. She's got her shirt tucked into a pair of leggings, and she's wearing a pair of flat canvas shoes. Pulling out her phone, she looks about to see if a teacher is watching. She catches my eye and, for the first time in years, she doesn't scowl or sneer. She just looks at me for a second like she wants to say something, then turns away.

"Come on, Betty," says Kat. "I want to hear about the *kissing*!"

For once, Mrs. P. turns up at just the right moment. "Blazers," she says, standing legs astride at the front of the stage, "*will* improve your exam results!" She spends the next five minutes defending this dubious statement. "As you all know," she says, flashing a brief smile to indicate she is changing the subject, "our Autumn Celebration is on Thursday evening."

Definitely hadn't forgotten about that.

"Joss Carlisle," she continues, "was supposed to be giving us a sneak preview of his street dance performance, but he fractured his coccyx—please stop snickering, sophomores, a coccyx is a small bone"—massively increased sniggering—"at the base of your *spine.* On Friday, Joss danced quite literally *in the street* and was struck with some force by a girl on a Micro scooter." Mrs. P. chooses to ignore the hysterical laughter that erupts. "Fortunately, another act has agreed to fill his spot. I'm told they were rehearsing all day yesterday, so please give a warm round of applause to Toby Gray and his band, the Vanilla Chinchillas!"

"What's going on, Betty?" asks Kat.

"I don't know," I say, and then I watch, confused, as Frank and Dexter appear from behind the curtain. Toby follows them and goes to the front of the stage and takes the mike off Mrs. P.

"Actually," he says, his deep voice filling the hall, "it's Vanilla Chinchilla."

"Why didn't you tell us?" Bea whispers.

"I don't know anything about this," I say. Why wasn't I at the rehearsal? How can you rehearse without your singer?

"You'd better go up," says Kat, nudging me.

I stand and awkwardly pick my way over bags and legs. "Sorry," I say. "Excuse me."

Suddenly, Pearl gets up from her seat and walks past me, head held high. She climbs up the steps at the side of the stage and stands next to Toby. He hands her the microphone, and their fingers meet for a second.

I watch, frozen to the spot.

People start to turn round and look at me.

"Betty Plum, what are you doing?" Mrs. P. walks toward me. "Sit down at once!"

But I don't sit down. I look at Pearl and Toby, hardly believing my eyes.

"Betty!" says Mrs. P. "I said, *sit down*."

Around me, students snigger, and as Toby strums the opening chords of "Shut Up!" I keep pushing my way along the row. I trip over a boy's foot and fall into the center aisle just as the drums and bass kick in. The familiar music sweeps through the hall, and the laughs around me get louder.

As Pearl's *X Factor* vocals boom from the speakers, I turn and walk away from them, straight out of the hall, ignoring Mrs. P.'s demands that I *sit back down at once*!

I let the huge double doors slam shut behind me, muffling Pearl's voice, but I can still hear her as I walk down the corridor, then out of the main entrance and straight along the driveway.

"Betty Plum, where are you going?"

Mrs. P. has followed me out of school and is trotting after me in her high heels.

"I'm going home," I yell over my shoulder, "and I'm *never* coming back!"

15.

Poo is standing in the doorway to my bedroom. "Can I get you a cup of tea? A hot-water bottle?"

"No," I mutter. Then I change my mind. "Actually . . . that would be nice."

I hear the door shut.

Mrs. P. told Dad that I had "absconded," and because he was in the middle of a job he sent Poo home to find out what was wrong with me. By the time she came round, I was in bed, curtains shut, duvet over my head. She tried talking to me, but I just pretended she wasn't there. Not to be deliberately mean to Poo—I'd have done the same to anyone—and I wasn't lying when I told Mrs. P. that I was never going back to school. How could I?

Now my heart is definitely broken. I can feel it.

My mind is trapped, running over and over the events

of the past few weeks, and every thought makes my heart break a little bit more. Too late, I see that Toby isn't a hot vampire; he's just pale and he has a mean smile. He isn't a rebel, either. He just makes nice things look ugly by spraying crappy cartoons on them. And he doesn't love me. I don't even think he likes me. This is what hurts the most.

"Here you are," says Poo. I hear a cup being put on my bedside table. Next she slips the hot-water bottle into my bed. I feel fur on my feet and wriggle back. "It's a raccoon," explains Poo. "I brought it for you. I thought you might like it. Sorry it's not a fox."

I peer down at my feet and see a big stripy tail.

"Thanks," I say. "I do like it."

Then Poo leaves me, and immediately my mind flashes back to the hall, and I hear everyone laughing as I stumble along the row, and I see Toby and Pearl standing side by side looking beautiful, dark, and mean.

"BABES!" yells a shrill voice. I struggle to work out where I am, and then I see the duvet over my head and feel a cold raccoon between my feet. I remember: I'm hiding in my bed and never going to school again.

The bed sinks as Kat plonks herself down by my knees. "We've got your bag," she says.

"Toby is such an *A-hole*," says Bea. "We've been ignoring him all day. Hey, are you coming out of there?"

I shake my head.

"Poor Betty," says Kat, and she pats my bottom. "Sorry. Thought that was your shoulder."

"We came to find you as soon as we got out of assembly," says Bea, "but you'd already gone home, and when we called Rue said you wouldn't talk."

"She told us to come over," says Kat. "That's okay, isn't it?"

Under the duvet, I nod.

"Hey, Betty," says Bea. "Why did Toby do that to you?"

"Because I'm such a bad kisser," I say, breaking my silence. It sounds so funny, I start to laugh and cry at the same time. Then I decide I might as well tell them the whole story, so I stick my head out of the duvet and start talking. "It's weird," I say, when I get to the bit where I left the party. "The more I got to know him, the less I liked him."

"Depleting hotness," says Kat, giving me another pat. "It's when you actually get turned off of someone the more you hang out with them."

"Just because someone's got a lovely bum doesn't mean they're lots of fun," adds Bea. "My nan told me that."

"I just wish he could have been nice," I say, "like . . ." I think about the boys in school, but I'm imagining someone much better.

"Bill!" says Kat. "He's definitely the nicest boy I've ever met . . . and he's got a *lush* bum."

"Kat!" yells Bea. "Don't talk about his *bottom*. Betty's like his sister."

"Seriously, I've seen it in a wet suit. He's ripped. . . . Did you know he's the captain of the T15 club and they won the championship?"

"Kat's been showing me YouTube videos of Bill all day," explains Bea. "She claims she's addicted."

"He's a good windsurfer," I say, and then I fall silent because, honestly, I didn't know he was the captain of the T15s. I don't even know what the T15s are. . . .

"Isn't he?" And Kat is off, describing mind-blowing "Vulcans" and back loops. "Next Saturday," says Kat, barely pausing for breath, "there's a sailing taster lesson, and we're going, aren't we, Bea?"

Bea nods. "Come with us, Betty," she says. "It'll be fun."

I imagine it. Just me and my best friends being stupid and laughing for hours.

"No thanks," I say.

I can't see a way of getting out of bed, let alone hanging out with my friends and being me again.

"Downstairs or up here?" asks Poo. She's standing at the door holding a plate of toast. "I've made you up a bed in the front room so you can watch TV."

It's Tuesday, and Dad's agreed that I can have another

couple of days off school. If I can stretch out my "illness" to Friday, I'll even miss the school concert. Dad's tried to tell me that leaving school forever isn't a viable option, but I still can't imagine going back. Today he's left Poo to look after me, which basically means "make sure Betty doesn't do anything insane." It's getting kind of stuffy in bed.

"*Bargain Hunt*'s just started," says Poo.

Wrapping my duvet around me, I follow her downstairs. There's a big pile of pillows on the sofa and a glass of water on the coffee table. Sitting on the top pillow is the hot-water bottle. Still wrapped in my duvet, I get on the sofa and push the raccoon down by my feet.

"Very warm," I say.

And that's how I find myself watching *Bargain Hunt* with Poo. At first we don't talk much, but when *Relocation, Relocation* comes on, I'm forced to agree when she says that Suzie from Wimbledon is a "spoiled little cow" and that she's totally "perving over Phil."

After lunch—grilled cheese—she says she's going to let me rest. "How are you feeling?" she asks.

"A bit better," I say.

"I might be able to help," she says. "I'm trained in Thai massage." She comes and perches on the edge of the sofa. "Tell me where it hurts."

I think about Toby gazing at Pearl, the way their fingers brushed as he handed her the microphone. Without warning, I see his naked chest with its four prominent hairs. I stare out the window. Then, for some reason, I picture Kat and Bill sitting on the beach together, a barbecue glowing in the background.

"It hurts here," I say to Poo, patting my chest. My heart thuds under my fingers. "It really aches."

"Shut your eyes," says Poo.

I do what I'm told and hear her moving around the room, adjusting the blinds. The sofa sinks down by my feet, and then I feel cold air as she pulls the duvet back. She starts massaging the bottom of my feet. It should be horrible, but it makes me feel sleepy. "I want you to imagine you are standing at a gate." Immediately I see a gate in front of me. It's green, a bit like Nanna and Gramps's gate. "You are stepping into a beautiful garden. You are surrounded by flowers, and your feet tread on soft, cool grass. Shut the gate behind you. Everything that is making you ache has to stay outside."

Poo is a nut, I think to myself. My dad has managed to get himself a nut of a girlfriend. But in my head I slam the gate shut on Pearl and Toby and turn into my amazing garden. Poo chatters on about the sun warming my face and pink blossoms and birds singing, all the time massaging my feet in tiny circles. Her story ends with me lying in an imaginary hammock, drifting off to sleep . . . and I really am sleepy.

"That was nice," I whisper. "Was that Thai massage?"

"Not really—just some crazy stuff I made up," she says as she covers up my feet. "Thought you'd like it."

Yep, I think as she slips out of the room. Definitely a nut. But kind of a nice nut.

16.

I spend Wednesday reading *The Secret Diary of Adrian Mole, Aged 13 and ¾* and eating toast. Rue's been given the day off.

That evening, I go back up to my room and get out Dennis and read through all of Mum's letters and Bill's poems, trying to work out how I could have got it so wrong about Toby. I take *The one where my heart was broken* out of the Puma box and hold it for a minute before resting it against Mum's picture. Then I feel like listening to a bit of Bettye, so I put on Mum and Dad's song, but, to be honest, the line "Kiss me each morning for a million years" probably isn't what I need to hear right now.

A *million* kisses? One was bad enough. The tears well up again, and I pull Mr. Smokey off my feet and hug him to me. He must be fed up with me snuffling into his fur because he squirms out of my arms, walks along my bookcase, then leaps onto my wardrobe. He sits up there and glares at me like I'm a stranger.

"Sorry," I say to him. "It's just I had a really bad first kiss."

"Meow," he says.

"Do you remember that time you'd been eating Whiskas Rabbit Supermeat and you accidentally put your tongue in my mouth? We were nuzzling and then you yawned?" I pause, but he doesn't reply. Like me, he's probably tried to block out the memory. "Well, *that* was better than my kiss with Toby."

I hear a knock at the door. "Come in," I say, lifting Mr. Smokey off the wardrobe.

"Who were you talking to?"

"Bill!" I say, turning round and clutching Mr. Smokey to me. I haven't changed out of my pajamas for three days. "I was talking to Mr. Smokey . . . the only man I trust in the whole world."

Bill's wearing a gray T-shirt I've never seen before. I wonder if he bought it to impress Kat. He does look quite impressive in it.

"Kat told me you were hiding in bed," he says, "so I thought I'd come and cheer you up."

"I only hid for a day."

Bill stands awkwardly in the middle of the room and then sits on the end of my bed. "She told me what Toby did."

"What exactly did she tell you?" If she told him about the four chest hairs or the disaster kiss, I will have to kill her.

"About what happened in assembly," he says.

I groan and flop back. "So now everyone knows I was publicly dumped." Mr. Smokey wriggles out of my arms and jumps back on the wardrobe.

"I brought you this," he says, pulling Eric's Shave a Sheep game out of his backpack. He knows it's my favorite Lego game.

"That's cool, Bill, but did Kat tell you I *fell over* . . . and basically Toby didn't want me in the band, because I'm so bad at *kissing*." Bill leans forward, rests his chin in his hands, and stares at the wardrobe. I don't blame him for not looking at me. I'm a disaster. "I'm never going back to school, Bill," I say. "I can't."

"Betty," he says, not taking his eyes off the wardrobe, "*you* are *amazing* and Toby is just not. You're a starry sky, and he's just someone gazing up at you."

Kat's right. Bill is the nicest boy in the world. Why couldn't I have gone out with someone like him?

I sit on my bed and hug my knees. Bill turns and looks at me. I see his frown, and his gray eyes that are exactly the same color as a stormy sea. Then something happens. Something totally unexpected. For the first time in my life, I see how gorgeous Bill's face is. Bill has a cutesome face! I'm so amazed, my mouth falls open.

"What?" he says, staring at me.

I shut my mouth and blink a few times. "Nothing," I say. "Just thinking about . . ." I look around the room. "This." I pick up Mum's letter from by my bed. "This is my *last one*."

"What do you mean?"

I tell Bill all about Mum's letters, about how she hid them in the attic for me and what she put in them. I say that for the first time in my life, I feel like I've got a mum, and I don't want to lose her just when I've found her. It's good to talk about the letters . . . and it stops me from staring at Bill's face.

"I'm scared of opening it," I say, holding it in my lap. "After this there's nothing left."

"Do you want another quotation?" Bill asks.

"No way. I'm never ever going out with anyone ever again."

"It's not about him," says Bill. "It's about your mum." I pass him Dennis and a felt-tip pen. He starts to write. "This is Shakespeare, and it's from his most famous love sonnet: 'Shall I Compare Thee to a Summer's Day.' "

"Bill, I said no love!"

"Wait," he says, and then he starts to write on a blank page. "This is what comes at the end of the poem: 'So long as men can breathe, or eyes can see, So long lives this, and this gives life to thee.' " He looks at me. "You see, your mum's letters mean you will always have her, and she will always have you. You've got her letters, so she's never going away."

I look at Mum's letter. I can't say anything. I pick up her photo. Her face beams with life. I've always been surrounded by pictures of Mum, but they didn't make her real. Her letters have made her real.

"Thanks, Bill," I say. "Your essay has been more helpful than you can imagine."

He laughs and opens Shave a Sheep, shaking the Lego bricks over my feet. "I'm pleased I could be of assistance," he says, then passes me the dice. "Are we playing evil rules?"

"No way," I say, looking down because Bill's eyes are doing funny things to my tummy. "We're playing anarchy rules."

"I'm going to whop your ass, Betty," he says. "I taught Kat to play the other night, and she beat me. I'm out for revenge on a girl."

"What?"

"I taught Kat to play. . . ." He looks up. "She came over to borrow an old wet suit."

They're sharing wet suits? Why shouldn't they share wet suits? Or cuddles . . . or kisses?

"Your go," I say, throwing the die at him.

He catches it with one hand. "We watched *Labyrinth*," he adds.

What? That is totally *our* film. It's about a goblin king stealing a baby, and we've watched it so many times together. I try to hide my jealousy.

"That's cool," I say.

It's not cool. It's the opposite of cool. I look at Bill through my bangs. He's concentrating on making wool for his sheep.

And that's the moment I realize I totally like Bill. And I mean *Flynn Rider* like. I fancy my best friend! He looks up at me. A burning blush creeps over my cheeks. In fact, so much blood is rushing to my face that I feel faint. Bill looks at me curiously. Nothing can hide my glowing cheeks . . . except for a cat jumping off a wardrobe and landing on my head!

"Best cat ever," I whisper into Mr. Smokey's fluffy tummy.

When Bill has gone—I beat him three times—confusing boy-thoughts ping-pong around in my head. Seeing Bill has done something to the ache. It's still there, but it's definitely losing its power. I feel much more like me.

In fact, I feel so much like me that I decide to do some Epic Silent Dancing. It's a good way to celebrate the discovery that Toby hasn't completely broken my heart.

I put my headphones on and find "I Like to Move It." I turn the volume up loud and—after checking there are no gaps in the curtains—I press play.

At first I just stand there. Then my hands start doing the Sprinkler, and my hips join in with some thrusting . . . and then I just can't stop myself. I Moonwalk toward Mr. Smokey, do some Hammer Time, and end up Kung Fu Fighting Toby's imaginary face. At the end of the song, I realize I'm smiling, so I Epic Silent Dance all over again.

Then, because I'm still smiling and because Betty is back, I realize I can read Mum's last letter and it will all be okay.

I pull off my headphones and pick up *The one where my heart was broken*. I drop down on my bed, heart thudding from the dancing, pajamas all sweaty, and I start to read.

Dear Plumface,

So here's how it happened. You remember my Werther's Originals kiss with Carlo? If not, you'd better open The one where I have my first kiss *because this is the sequel.*

Read it? Good.

The day after the kiss, Carlo and I arranged to go on a secret walk. I barely slept that night. We met at the pier, really early, and wandered along the seafront and up onto the Downs. As soon as we got into the countryside, Carlo held my hand. It was even better than I had imagined it would be. Eventually, we climbed down a ladder to this secret bit of beach that you can get to only when the tide is out. We lay on the rocks, the sun warming our faces, and talked for hours.

Then we had the picnic I'd brought. I can still remember what I grabbed before I left the house: cheese sandwiches, banana milk, one bag of chips, and half an Easter egg. When the tide was lapping at the bottom of our rock, we climbed back up the ladder. Carlo pulled me up the last few steps.

It was the perfect first date.

Because I was sure that's what it was: our first date. Carlo never said anything, like, "I love you. Will you go out with me?" I guessed that was because Eleanor was our friend, and he knew he had to split up with her.

But as we left the countryside and started to walk along roads, past cars and people, I realized something had changed. Carlo let go of my hand and moved farther away from me. Then, when I fell off the curb, he didn't laugh. Usually he laughed all the time, especially if I did something silly.

"So . . ." I said when we got to my road.

"So," he said, looking just over my shoulder. "See you at school?"

All evening, I tried to explain away his behavior. I knew it must be hard for him. He'd been Eleanor's boyfriend for so long—he wouldn't want to upset her. Although, really, she wasn't the world's greatest person. When our class were filling shoe boxes up with Christmas presents for children in orphanages, she said she didn't see the point of doing it "for Romanian kids."

After a night of worrying, I went to school and I found Carlo and Eleanor hugging outside the main entrance. Not in an "it's over" type of way, more in an "I totally love you, let me press into your entire body" type of way. Carlo looked across at me. He was sending me a message.

That's when my heart was broken. I was sure he had chosen Eleanor over me because something about me wasn't right. I just wasn't good enough for him. I spent hours trying to work out what it was. Maybe I wasn't pretty enough, or clever enough . . . had I said something stupid? It was only years later that I realized that I'd got it all wrong: It was Carlo who wasn't good enough for me.

Now, Betty, I have to confess something. The one where I fall in love . . . *isn't an entirely truthful title. I should have called it* The one where I thought I'd fallen in love. . . . *You see, sometimes, when you think you've fallen in love, you haven't, not really. It's only when you truly fall in love that you know what love is. I didn't want to put that in the letter, because you might have thought I was being patronizing, a bit* Cheer up, love. There are plenty more fish in the sea.

I will put one more letter in the attic, and it will be called True Love. *I'll put it in a Quality Street tin. Save it for when you hit the jackpot, for when you meet someone who loves you for who you are and who would never settle for anyone else, particularly someone who hated Romanian orphans. You'll know when to read the letter because true love feels like coming home.*

The other reason it's in a separate place is because it really is my last letter. I don't want you to open it unless it's absolutely the right time. I realize these letters might be hard to read. Sometimes they've been hard to write. I'd like to keep writing them forever, but I've run out of time. Even Dad, Nanna, and Auntie Kate know that now. I'm leaving hospital this afternoon, and I won't come back. Usually going home is a good thing, but not for me. Everyone's finally accepted that I'm never getting better and that there's nothing anyone can do except wait, and I don't want to wait in hospital. I want to be at home, with you and Dad.

One day, if someone does break your heart and makes you feel small and insignificant, I want you to remember this: When you were a tiny person, not even two years old, you were so mighty and amazing that you kept me alive. Today, it is you, *Betty, who is making my heart beat, my lungs fill with air, and my fingers hold this pen. Just so I can leave hospital today and hold you in my arms again.*

Love you always,
Mumface xxx

Carefully, I put the letter into Dennis. My throat aches. I wish I could tell Mum that I found her letters and read them, that I've felt how much she loved me. When I called my sketchbook the Big Book of Love, I was thinking about Toby, but as I turn over each page, making sure Mum's letters are in place and reading Bill's quotations, I realize that this book isn't about Toby at all.

But it is about love.

It's about me falling in love with two people who've always been in my life, waiting for me: Bill and my mum.

Mum is right. I wasn't really in love with Toby. I didn't feel at home with him, more like I was on another planet. When I'm with Bill, I can be me. I need to tell Bill that I got it massively wrong, but what if I've left it too late? What if Bill and Kat got together when I was in a garage gazing at Toby, playing *FIFA 14* and learning to sing miserable?

I lost the chance to be with my mum, and now I'm losing Bill, too. And this time it's all my fault!

Before I go to sleep, I turn on my phone and delete Toby's messages. There are only seven. I've had more texts from Verizon. Finally, I wipe his phone number.

I'm about to turn off my phone when I get a new message. It's from Bill: **Just saw this and thought of you.** There's a photo attached. Obviously, I can't see it. I can't think what to say to him, so I just leave the phone by my bed and wait for the picture to come through.

As I drift off to sleep, I think about Mum and Bill. It's good knowing that *True Love* is up in the attic waiting for me. Then I think about Bill's lines of poetry, about the night I slept in his bed and how he said something important to me, something that is hidden just out of reach. Whatever it is, I think it might be the answer to everything.

17.

When I wake up, the room is bright and I can't hear any sounds in the house. Dad must have gone to work. I lie in bed, staring at the sunlight streaming through the gap at the bottom of the curtains. It's making stripy lines across my legs. Dreamily I realize that today is the day of the Autumn Celebration. Then, as I'm curled up, all warm and sleepy, I suddenly remember what Bill said to me.

When I stayed the night at his house, and I was half-asleep, half-awake, just like now, I asked him how his essay was going. He laughed, and he said, "*Betty, there's never been an essay.*"

But if there was no essay, why did he have his love-poetry book all highlighted and studied? I sit up so fast, the blood rushes from my head and I feel dizzy. Bill told me why: He said when he read the poems, he thought about *me*. He said it in his sarcastic voice, but what if he was telling the truth and wanted to hide it? After all, I'd just been going on and on about how much I wanted to kiss Toby.

I grab Dennis. I'm not the best at English because, although I love reading, I hate analyzing. It ruins the story. But this time, I think it might make the story.

So I can weigh up all the evidence, I draw another love grid in Dennis, and I do it just like my English teacher has taught me:

EVIDENCE:	EXPLAIN:
"She walks in beauty like the night of cloudless climes and starry skies"	He's talking about me! He thinks I am as beautiful as a starry night. I <u>do</u> have a lot of freckles.
"Love is like a child that longs for every thing it can come by"	Bill went to Brighton with my friends because he thought he might get to see me for just five minutes.
"But one man loved the pilgrim soul in you"	Bill totally <u>gets</u> me—the way I love cycling down hills, how I like my jam spread to the edges of my toast, and why I find the word <u>furry</u> funny.

"I have spread my dreams under your feet; Tread softly because you tread on my dreams"	Just after he wrote this on my arm, he told me he wasn't writing an essay. He was saying, I'm about to lay my heart at your feet, Betty, so don't go and do a Riverdance on it.
"So long as men can breathe, or eyes can see, So long lives this, and this gives life to thee"	Okay, strictly speaking, this was about Mum, but what if this is the final clue? Bill is just waiting for me to use my eyes, read his quotes, and see what he's been trying to tell me.

Dennis has been about Bill and me since I first wrote the words *she walks in beauty like the night* and surrounded it with doodles of silver stars, but Toby's smile was so dazzling, I couldn't see it.

But what if I'm just twisting Bill's words? In my last report, my teacher did say my English work was "wildly imaginative." I pull out my phone. I need to see Bill's photo.

I open the text, and slowly the image appears. First, I see a plastic moon hanging from a ceiling. It's Eric's ceiling—I can tell by the hot-chocolate spray marks that I was partly responsible for. Next, Eric's blurred face appears. It looks like he's jumping on his bed and his hair is shooting up, defying gravity. Then I see stars. Dangling from the moon, bumping Eric on the head, are around twenty blue, green, and yellow stars. It's a starry sky.

A starry sky that made him think of me!

Something inside me glows with excitement, but I force myself to calm down. Could *Eric* have reminded Bill of me? Am I like a six-year-old boy who smells a bit like a hamster? There's only one way I can find out. I have to see Bill. Surely, when I look at him I'll be able to tell if he's secretly been fancying me for weeks? Then, if I'm right, I'll prove to him that I'm totally over Toby and that I've finally seen what's been in front of me all this time. It's going to have to be something big. This isn't the sort of thing you can fix with cupcakes or a cuddly toy.

By the time I've had a shower—my first in three days—dried my hair, and eaten two bowls of Rice Krispies, I've come up with a plan. Before I do anything, I've got to speak to Kat. There are only so many times you can steal Jesus before your friend gives up on you.

She answers her phone immediately. "Aren't you supposed to be in geography?" I say.

"I am," she says, "but Kabir just made Mrs. Ledger cry by pretending she'd become invisible. She ran out and hasn't come back. Are you feeling better?"

"I'm fine . . . really surprisingly fine," I say, "but I've two important things to ask you."

"Okay, but speak up. Kabir's put a violent film on the interactive whiteboard."

I take a deep breath. "Do you like Bill?" I ask.

The line goes quiet. I hear a scream followed by a massive explosion.

"I like him," Kat says, "and he is ten out of ten, but I don't *like* him."

"But you said he was ripped and his bum looked lush . . . and that you were *addicted*."

"To *windsurfing*. It's addictive. Honestly, Betty, the whole world doesn't revolve around boys." Her words make me grin. "Bill is awesomely ripped, but he's not interested in me, and that's sort of lessened the impact of his hotness. Plus there's this other instructor, Rob, and he's got these arms like—"

"Listen, Kat, I've got to do something very important, and I haven't got time to hear about Rob's arms."

"They're like Spider-Man's," she blurts out. "Go on, next question. Make it quick because I can hear a walkie-talkie. Mrs. P. is approaching."

So I ask my next question and, amazingly, she agrees. She really is the most incredible friend.

It's one o'clock, and the Autumn Celebration starts in five hours. I have to see Bill if I'm going to put my plan in action. I'm not sure what I'll say—I just hope that when I look at him somehow I'll be able to tell if he likes me or not, if I've put the clues together right, or if I've been a total idiot for the second time this week.

There is one problem. Today is Thursday, the day when everyone at Bill's school does an enrichment activity. Bill always goes windsurfing at his club in Eastbourne with other boys in his year. If I leave now, I might get there in a couple of hours. I haven't got a clue which bus I need or where it will drop me off. I don't care. I'm on a mission . . . a love mission!

After a quick trip up to the attic, I grab my panda hat, my purse, and my phone. Then I tug on my yellow DMs. I scribble a note for Dad: *Decided to go to school after all. It's the Autumn Celebration tonight. You and Rue should come—6:00. X Betty* I slap it on the fridge, holding it in place with the potato magnet.

Then I kiss Mr. Smokey good-bye, and I'm out of the door and booking it to the bus stop.

18.

"Where's the sea?" I ask the bus driver. I've arrived in Eastbourne, but I haven't got a clue where to go. The bus has dropped me in the town center.

"That way. You can't miss it." I run down the road she pointed out, dashing past charity shops, bakers, and gift shops. Soon I'm standing next to the pier. I look left and right. The seafront stretches away in both directions. Even though it's nearly winter, the sun is shining and the boardwalk is busy with foreign students and old ladies in pastel anoraks who are being blown about by the wind. I don't know which way to go.

I run onto the pier and look right. I see hotels, the gentle dip of the Downs, and, in the distance, white cliffs. The dark sea is churning below me, covered in waves that peak and spray in all directions. I can't see any windsurfers.

I go to the other side of the pier and grip the railing. I feel the peeling paint digging into my palms. Then, between two waves, I spot them: a group of windsurfers, their triangular sails zigzagging across the sea.

I run off the pier just as a mini train pulls up. The tiny cars are packed with retired vacationers. I pay the driver two pounds, and soon I'm squeezed between two elderly gentlemen who are both wearing tracksuits.

"In a rush?" asks Red Tracksuit. I don't know what gives me away; perhaps it's the way I'm muttering, "C'mon, c'mon," under my breath as the driver checks each door and chats about the "glorious sunshine" with every passenger.

"I'm going to see a friend," I say, "but I'm not sure I'm going to catch him in time."

"Ohh!" says Blue Tracksuit. "A feller . . . you like him, do you?"

"Yes," I say, "but I don't know if he likes me." Why am I telling them this? "You see, he's been my friend for years."

"Don't worry," says the lady sitting opposite me. She leans forward and pats my arm. "That's the best basis for marriage."

"Thanks," I say, "but I'm only fifteen." The mini train starts to hum and then slowly creeps forward, and I mean *slowly*. "A boyfriend would be nice," I add.

"Then let's go get 'im," says Blue Tracksuit, really quite loudly.

"Wahoo!" yells Red Tracksuit, punching the air. The train picks up speed, and soon the whole carriage is whooping and clapping as we race along at five miles an hour. I glance at my phone: 3:24 p.m. A woman in a mobility scooter overtakes us. We really do need to get moving.

The train stops outside a wooden building where a Spray Watersports flag is whipping in the wind. Immediately, I spot the Cardinal Heanan minibus in the parking lot. My hands are shaking so much that I can't open the train door. My fellow passengers all have arthritic fingers, so the driver has to let me out.

"Good luck, Betty!" shouts Red Tracksuit as I run toward Spray, and soon the whole carriage joins in. The driver encourages the hysteria by giving me three blasts of the train whistle. I wave over my shoulder and scramble up a bank of pebbles.

Rounding the corner of the building, I see a group of boys my age leaning on a veranda railing, staring out to sea. The windsurfers are still out there, black silhouettes that skim over the waves so quickly they barely make contact with the sea.

I turn to the boy nearest to me. "Do you know where Bill is?" I ask.

"On the water," he says. "He was the only one allowed to go out."

"Out there?" I squint, trying to work out which of the black shapes Bill might be, but they are way too far away, and the waves keep rising up and hiding the windsurfers from my view. "Is it safe?" The waves seem to be swallowing them up.

"Depends how good you are," says the boy. "Bill's good."

"Which one is he?"

"That one," he says. "With red stripes on the sail."

I walk down the beach, slipping over pebbles, all the time trying to keep my eye on Bill's red sail. I watch him flip up on a wave and turn 360 degrees before crashing down into the sea and dipping below the surface. In seconds he's up again, heading toward the horizon. He is good. Why didn't I know how well he could do this? I sit down on the beach and watch him as he flies over the sea. Even with my zero knowledge of windsurfing, I can tell he's one of the best.

A van pulls up behind me. I turn as a man jumps out. When I look back at the sea, I can't see Bill. Desperately I study each sail in turn. Then I see someone coming in, sailing straight onto the pebbles and jumping off his board at the last minute.

The sail has red stripes. I peer at the person hauling the board out of the water. He starts to walk in my direction. Then I see blond hair and a serious expression that makes my tummy flip.

Suddenly, I'm not sure I want to know if he likes me,

and I'm scared. What if he looks at me in horror? What if he laughs at me? Could we ever be friends again?

C'mon, Betty, I tell myself, *you can't put this off.* I'm just about to call out his name when he stops and puts down his board.

I watch as he unzips his wet suit to the waist. Slowly, he peels the wet black fabric off his arms, letting the top half fall down round his waist. I stare at Bill's naked chest. His hot naked chest.

I look down, cheeks flaming, heart racing. *This* I was not expecting. Is this chest-love or chest-fear? Has Toby made me fear chests?

Even though my face is burning, I force myself to glance back up at Bill. I think it's important to confront your fears. He picks up his board and sail and walks up the beach, heading straight for me. No. I'm definitely not scared of Bill's muscular, well-defined, broad-shouldered chest. In fact, I'm sort of the opposite of scared. I'm more *loving* it.

I want to hide, to give myself time to compose myself, to get over the discovery that I completely and madly like my best friend. Unfortunately, I'm sitting in the middle of a huge pebbly beach. Quickly, I shove my head in my duck backpack, pretending to rummage for something. Bill might not see me.

"Betty?"

Oh, bum. He must have recognized the enormous orange beak.

"Bill!" I pull my head out of the bag and smile up at him. *Focus on his face, Betty, focus on his face.*

"What are you doing here?" he asks.

Really good question. "Well, you see . . ." I say, scrambling to my feet, "I wanted to invite you to the Autumn Celebration at my school tonight."

"So you came all the way to Eastbourne to do it?"

"Um, yeah." He frowns at me. *The face, Betty, do not lower your gaze.* I'm really not getting any massive love vibes from Bill, more total confusion vibes. I thought everything would be much clearer. "You see, we need to go now, or we'll miss it."

"And it's really important that I go to this thing at your school?" says Bill, smiling.

That smile is ten out of ten. How could I not have seen it before? "It really is the most important thing in the world," I say, looking into his eyes. We're standing about a meter apart. His hair is dripping, and his chest is still totally and utterly naked. I want him to put his board down and wrap his arms round me.

"Then let's go," he says, turning and climbing up the bank of pebbles. "I'll see if I can get you a seat on the minibus."

19.

"Come on," I say to Bill, running up the steps to school. "It's about to start." Avoiding the main entrance to the hall, I lead Bill down a side corridor to a door that opens near the stage. I hold it open and peer inside. The hall is almost full, crowded with parents and students, but I spot an empty seat between two mums. "Sit there," I say, pushing him forward.

"In the front row?"

"I want you to have a good view," I say. He slips into the seat just as the lights go down. Mrs. P. steps onto the stage. "Look out for my dad," I whisper.

Now I need to find Kat so she can convince me I'm doing the right thing. When I explained my plan to her, I imagined I'd have talked to Bill. Instead, I've been sitting on a minibus, sandwiched between two sophomore boys having a conversation about tides. Bill wasn't allowed to sit with me, because his teacher assumed I was his girlfriend and wanted to make sure we didn't get up to any "hanky-panky."

I find Kat in a practice room, tuning her guitar. "Betty," she cries. "Thank God you're here."

"Is this madness?" I ask, shrugging off my coat. "Tell me I'm doing the right thing, Kat."

"I'm about ninety-nine percent certain that you're doing the right thing," she says, coming over to help me when I get my zip stuck in my hair. "And, yes, it's madness. That's why it's a great idea."

"You've got the music?"

"And I've been rehearsing for the past hour." She runs through a series of chords while I pull off my sweater and wriggle out of my jeans. "You appear to be getting undressed, Betty."

"Hang on," I say, rummaging around in my backpack. "Is this beyond madness?" I hold up a white minidress.

"Yes," she says, grinning. "Which is why you should definitely wear it."

I slip the dress over my head. It fits me like a glove.

"It's one of Mum's costumes from when she was in the Swanettes," I say. I smooth the fabric over my hips and tug down the hem. I pull on my DMs. "How do I look?"

Kat looks at me carefully. "Stunning," she says finally.

"Although Mrs. P. will have a cow when she sees the length of that skirt."

Just then, an eighth-grade boy sticks his head around the door. "You're next," he says.

My stomach churns. "I don't know if I can do it, Kat," I say. "I keep thinking about the last time I was in the hall, when everyone laughed at me."

"Come on," she says, grabbing her guitar and my hand. "Last time you ran away. This is totally different." She pulls me out into the corridor. "Plus, you owe me, big-time."

She leads me to the side of the stage, and we stand in the shadows, watching a girl play her flute. All around us are groups of students who are either waiting to perform or hanging around to watch the acts. Kat squeezes my hand. I look up. On the other side of the stage is Toby, his arm draped over Pearl's shoulder. Standing beside them are Bollie. Bea lifts up one hand, tucks her thumb in, and wiggles four fingers at me. I return the wave, and we smile. I look back at Toby. Funny. He doesn't look so tall and handsome anymore. More lanky and a bit of an idiot.

I look at Pearl, and she fixes her eyes on me before turning away and staring at the flute girl. Applause sweeps the hall.

"Thank you, Ellie," says Mrs. P. "That was *haunting*. And now, please welcome onstage"—there is a pause while she consults her clipboard—"Kat Knightley and . . . Betty Plum." She frowns as she reads my name.

"Come on," says Kat, pulling me forward. I follow her onto the stage and pick up the microphone while she plugs her guitar into the amp. The applause dies out and is replaced by an awkward silence. I stare into the depths of the hall, looking at the rows and rows of upturned faces. A light shines in my eyes, and the audience shuffles around. I know that Toby and Pearl are watching, maybe Dad and Rue, and that Bill is sitting in the front row.

"Before we begin," I say. My voice is a whisper, so I pull the mike closer. "I want to say something." Mrs. P. looks at me from her place in the front row with narrowed eyes. "I am going to sing a song called 'Then You Can Tell Me Goodbye' by Bettye Swann." There are coughs and whispers from the audience. I ignore them and carry on. "I'm singing this for my mum because she loved this song—" I look down at the front row, blinking into the spotlight, until I find Bill. He's sitting forward, his chin resting on his hands. He's watching me intently.

I turn away from Bill and look straight ahead. "And I'm singing it for my friend, Bill, because . . . I love him." There's a moment of silence, and then gasps and giggles surround me, but they're drowned out by Kat playing the opening of the song. Her notes are true and clear, and as the melody fills the hall, I grip the mike. I've done it now. The worst is over.

And maybe it's because Kat is so good, or maybe it's because the sight of me in a white minidress, Panda hat, and yellow DMs is so strange, but the hall falls silent. My skin tingles from my head to my toes as I wrap my fingers tightly around the mike.

Then I shut my eyes, and I sing my love song to Mum and Bill. And it feels so right that I relax and just let the song pour out of me.

The music dies away as I sing the last words. The hall is quiet, and then the clapping starts. I'm still clutching the mike, too scared to look down at Bill, and Kat takes it out of my hands and puts it back in the stand. Then we walk off the stage.

Toby and his band brush past us, Pearl trailing behind them.

"Hang on," I say to Kat. "I want to watch this." I'm feeling so brave now. They start setting up, and Pearl takes my place at the mike. Kat and I stand with Bea, and the three of us hold hands.

Soon, they are ready. As Mrs. P. introduces them, Pearl turns away from the audience and peers into the shadows. She's looking for someone: She's looking for me. When she finds me standing between Kat and Bea, I refuse to look away. Her face is hard, and her makeup is heavy. As she stares at me, the band starts playing. In my head, I count down the seconds to her first line.

At the last moment, she turns away from me, faces the audience, and then, just when she should start singing, she drops the mike on the floor and walks toward the steps at the front of the stage. First, Toby stops playing, and then Dexter and Frank catch on, and the music stops abruptly.

"What're you doing?" Toby calls out as Pearl walks down the stairs.

"Shut up!" she yells over her shoulder, and then she walks straight out of the hall.

For the rest of the concert, I hide in the practice room, and at the end I make the others leave without me. I don't want them around when I see Bill . . . if he's waited for me. Eventually, the janitor kicks me out, saying it's time to lock up. I get my things together and open the door next to the stage—the door I pushed Bill through—and peer into the hall. The strip lights are on, and a harsh light fills the room.

It's empty.

Stomach churning, I grip my backpack straps and head for the main exit. Outside, I stand at the top of the steps. A few students are still around, loading instruments into the back of parents' cars, chatting and calling out to one another.

Behind me, the door opens, and Toby backs out carrying one of Dexter's drums. He stops when he sees me. There's a moment when neither of us speaks.

"You were epic, B-Cakes," he says, and then he walks over to his mum's sports car.

"Sorry I'm late," she says, leaning out of the window. "Did I miss it?"

"You didn't miss anything," he says.

Mrs. P. walks up the steps. "Well done, Betty," she says, slapping her clipboard against her hand. "A beautiful performance, really lovely."

"Thank you, Mrs. P," I say.

"I believe someone is waiting for you," she adds, nodding in the direction of the drive. And then I see Bill. He's leaning against the gatepost, arms folded, as if he's got all the time in the world. "Off you go," says Mrs. P. "Some of us have homes to go to."

I walk toward him, grateful that it's so dark. My cheeks burn, and my heart thuds in my chest.

He straightens up when he sees me, and I stop in front of him.

"Hello," I say.

"Hello," he replies. Then he smiles, and I have to hide my face bchind my hands.

I peek through my fingers. "So what did you think?" I ask.

"Well, Kat was a bit slow on the second verse," he says, "but she managed to catch up. . . . You, on the other hand . . . you were perfect."

"Really?"

"Betty," he says, "I was rocked by your love."

I step into his arms and rest my head on his chest. I feel

his heart through his T-shirt, and I close my eyes. I know I've come home. After a moment, I say, "That's another quotation, isn't it?"

"A bit of Sappho and a bit of me," he says. "You know, Betty, you could have told me what you felt on the beach . . . or the other day at your house . . . or even just sent me a text."

"Or maybe I could have dropped hints through mysterious lines of poetry. . . ."

"My own words weren't good enough," he says, and he rests his cheek on my head.

"This is a big hug," I say into his T-shirt.

"I've been waiting to do this for a long time."

"How long?"

"About two years." So Bill and I stand there, under a starry sky, and we don't need to say anything, because our hug says it all.

Eventually, we wander home, and Bill tells me about the awkward conversation he had with Dad and Rue, and how Rue took Dad off to the pub to recover from the shock of hearing me sing.

At my door, we face each other, and I know from all the movies I've watched and all the books I've read that this is the moment when we should kiss.

"There's something I need to tell you," I say. The lights are on in the house, so Dad and Rue must be home.

"What?"

"Basically," I say, looking at a hedge rather than at Bill, "I'm scared of kissing."

He laughs. "That's okay. We can do something else."

"Like what?" Suddenly I'm a bit alarmed.

"Something like"—he thinks for a second—"high fives!" He raises his hand, and our hands slap together, but we don't let go. We leave our fingers entwined.

Bill walks backward down the steps, still holding my hand. "Who wants to do kissing?" he says. "Yuck."

"Thanks, Bill," I say.

"Don't thank me," he says. "You've got me out of an embarrassing situation."

"One last high five for the road?"

"Let's make it a long, lingering one."

After three more high fives, I let myself into the house, shut the door, and rest my back against it. All I can do is grin.

I stick my head into the kitchen.

"Hey," I say.

Rue and Dad look up from the table. They're having a cup of tea. "There she is," says Dad. "My little girl . . . wearing the shortest skirt in the world."

"Sorry if I surprised you, Dad," I say. "I mean, I wanted you to be surprised, but in a good way."

"It was definitely good," says Rue. "Wasn't it?" She nudges Dad.

"Yes, good," he says. "And a bit freaky."

"Listen," I say. "I've got to go up into the attic."

"Tonight?"

"Yes, Dad, it's very important. . . . It's to do with true love."

"All right," he says. "Just watch where you tread. I don't want you coming through the ceiling."

"Why not take a hot chocolate up there," says Rue, getting to her feet. "And wear a sweater. It's going to be chilly."

Getting a mug of hot chocolate and a cat up a ladder is dangerous, but I manage it. After a few minutes of searching, I find the Quality Street tin. There's nothing inside except one purple envelope and the faint smell of Christmas chocolates. *True Love* is written on the envelope. I sit down with Mr. Smokey on my lap. Then, after I've had a sip of my drink, I open the envelope and pull out one folded sheet of paper.

Dear Plumface,

True love . . . has Dad told you about the Falling Star, and the moment we first set eyes on each other? Here's how I remember it.

It was a hot evening, and I was singing with the Swanettes in this pub in the depths of the countryside. We were stuck inside, performing our set to a handful of old boys. It was such a warm evening, the doors were all propped open and, as the sun set, moths found their way in and batted around my face. Just as I was singing the opening of "Then You Can Tell Me Goodbye," this tall blond man walks in, ducking down to avoid hitting his head on a beam. He looked at me, and I looked at him—our eyes literally met across a semicrowded room. If I'm honest, I wouldn't describe it as love at first sight—your dad has got pointy ears and oddly small hands, but his eyes . . . they were the kindest eyes I had ever seen.

After my set, your dad and I sat out in the beer garden until we were the only ones left, except for the cows in the next field, and told each other what we'd been doing with our lives while we were waiting to meet each other. When I got back to my B and B, I couldn't sleep. I was so excited about my future with pointy-eared Nick Plum. At six in the morning, I crept outside and sat on a wet bench in the garden. Birds were singing all around me. It felt like the world was just beginning. I had to tell someone how happy I was, so I went into the village, found a phone booth, and called up Nanna and told her I'd fallen in love. She said, "Are you drunk, Lorna?" then hung up.

I was head over heels in love. But, you know what, Betty? Your dad was just a warm-up act for the big one . . . for you.

When I first held you in my arms, all hot and pink, staring up at me with those dark eyes, I was overwhelmed with the biggest, craziest love ever. I held you close so you wouldn't feel scared—after all, you'd just popped into the world, and you looked quite annoyed about it.

"Hello, Betty Plum," I said. You scowled and opened your fingers like a starfish. "I'm Lorna Plum. I'm your mum, and I love you." You looked a bit like you didn't believe me, so I added, "Really. I'm going to look after you forever."

I thought I would look after you forever, Betty. I am so sorry.

You are lying next to me as I write this, fast asleep. Dad lifted you out of your cot and put you next to me. You've pushed your foot against my arm. It is smooth and strong and warm. Your face is red, and your hair is stuck to your cheek. In a moment, I'm going to put this letter in its envelope, seal it, and then put it in the box with all my other stuff that's waiting to go up to the attic. Then I am going to lie so close to you that I can feel your breath on my face and see your chest move up and down. I'm going to watch you until I fall asleep.

When we were sitting in the garden of the pub, Dad

told me that the stars in the sky aren't all there, that some have died and what we can see is their light that has just reached us. I hope my love has reached you, Betty.

You see, these letters were never supposed to be my good-bye. They are my hello.

Hello, Betty Plum, I'm your mum and I love you.

Always.

Mumface xx

20.

"Tack, Betty, tack!" yells Bill as the wind hits the sail, swinging it round in my direction.

"What?" I say, then I'm smacked in the face by a metal boom and flipped out of the boat and into the lake. Quickly, I shut my eyes and mouth. I know the drill. This is the fifth time it's happened today, but even so I manage to swallow some smelly water. I feel Bill's arms pulling me to the surface.

"I'm fine," I gasp, clinging to the side of the boat. I pull some seaweed out of my hair. "Just got to catch my breath."

I hang on while Bill does something involving a line and a cringle. I really wasn't listening when the instructor was explaining it all. Kat's right. Bill does look ripped in a wet suit. It's very distracting.

"Bea, you loser!" yells Kat. Their boat flies past us,

heading for a collision with a small boy who's learning to windsurf. It's too windy for us to go out on the sea today, so all the beginners have ended up on a lake in the middle of a park.

"Sorry!" shouts Bea as the boy flies into the water. He'll be okay. The water's not deep.

"Ready to come up?" asks Bill.

"Yep," I heave myself against the side of the boat, and Bill pulls me under my arms.

"C'mon," says Bill. "You've got to help me." I push hard against the slushy bottom of the lake and suddenly shoot out of the water, landing heavily on Bill. The boat sinks low and then bobs back up.

We laugh and then, because I want to and because he's quite simply my best friend in the whole world, I kiss him. He kisses me back and I taste salt and Mars bar, and the boat slowly turns in the water.

"Hey," I say, looking down at him, "we just kissed!"

"High five," says Bill, and our hands meet. I wrap my fingers round his. I never want to let go. "Hang on," he says, wriggling out of my grasp. He looks at me intently, then rubs his thumb across my cheek. "Swan poo," he explains. "Now . . . where were we?"

THANK YOU FOR READING THIS FEIWEL AND FRIENDS BOOK.

THE FRIENDS WHO MADE

POSSIBLE ARE:

JEAN FEIWEL
publisher

LIZ SZABLA
editor in chief

RICH DEAS
senior creative director

HOLLY WEST
associate editor

DAVE BARRETT
executive managing editor

ANNA ROBERTO
associate editor

CHRISTINE BARCELLONA
associate editor

EMILY SETTLE
administrative assistant

ANNA POON
editorial assistant

Follow us on Facebook or visit us online at mackids.com.

OUR BOOKS ARE FRIENDS FOR LIFE